# PURRFECTLY CLUELESS

## THE MYSTERIES OF MAX 12

## NIC SAINT

PUSS IN PRINT PUBLICATIONS

**PURRFECTLY CLUELESS**

**The Mysteries of Max 12**

Copyright © 2019 by Nic Saint

Edited by Chereese Graves

www.nicsaint.com

Give feedback on the book at: info@nicsaint.com

facebook.com/nicsaintauthor
@nicsaintauthor

First Edition

Printed in the U.S.A

# CHAPTER 1

*I* watched on with a modicum of weariness and exasperation as my human packed her weekend bag. Usually when Odelia goes on a trip she cordially invites me and Dooley along with her, and sometimes even Harriet and Brutus. Now, she was going away for the weekend and I wasn't invited!

Odelia was in no frame of mind to discuss what was obviously a grave oversight on her part. She was frowning so furiously I thought those grooves lining her brow would become permanently etched into her fair skin.

"Lemme see," she muttered. "Toiletries, check, phone charger, check, laptop and charger, check…" She heaved a deep sigh and her eyes flicked to her wardrobe. "Chase!" she suddenly cried. "Chase—where are you?!"

"What's wrong, babe?" Chase asked, as he came running.

She flapped her arms like a chicken. "I have nothing to wear!"

Chase heaved a sigh of relief. "I thought you were in trouble."

"I am in trouble! I'm going to spend the weekend with the

most gorgeous, most successful, most iconic actresses of our time and I've got nothing to wear!"

Chase moved over to the closet and gave it a critical look. He let his hand trail along the outfits. "You've got plenty of stuff, honey. Any of these will do."

She gave him a scathing look, the kind that says: of course you would say a dumb thing like that. You're a guy!

"I need my mom," she said, and Chase left the room, realizing he didn't fit that particular description. Moments later, Odelia opened the bedroom window and hollered, "Mom! I need you in here! Now!"

It was a testament to her nervous condition that she would resort to shouting at her mother like that. Usually Odelia is the most mild-mannered human any cat could ever hope to be adopted by. Today she was giving every indication of being on the verge of a nervous breakdown.

Like Chase, I decided to return downstairs. Things were looking pretty grim, and I needed my best buddy to confide in and commiserate with.

Dooley watched me descend the stairs with a hopeful look on his face. But when he caught my expression that hope was quickly squashed like a bug.

"No dice?" he asked, just to be sure.

"No dice," I confirmed. "She's not taking us and that's her final word." And even if I wanted to try and convince her, I knew from long association with Odelia that now wasn't the time. "She's having trouble packing," I explained as I took position next to Dooley on the couch. "Doesn't know what to wear."

"Oh," he said, immediately understanding.

"Yeah."

"So that's that, then."

"That's that," I agreed.

We both stretched out on the couch and stared before us, musing about what could have been.

Marge came in through the sliding glass door and directed an anxious look at us. I said, "Nothing to wear," and Marge immediately understood, for she nodded once, plastered a look of determination on her face and proceeded up the stairs.

Odelia has always been a nervous packer, and now, with her star-studded weekend coming up, things were even worse than usual. For a reporter this is a highly unusual situation, you might say, but then Odelia is not one of your globe-trotting reporters who practically live in their suitcases. She doesn't traverse the Sahel in a beat-up Jeep with only a toothbrush and her wits. She doesn't look to interview rebels in the jungles of war-torn Angola. She's a small-time reporter for a small-town rag called the *Hampton Cove Gazette*, so she hardly does any traveling at all. This weekend was an exception, therefore, and I could see why this would exacerbate the situation to the point she needed her mother to help negotiate the packing of her weekender case.

Next to us, Chase had also taken a seat, and now the three of us were waiting, like expectant parents awaiting news from the maternity ward, or the Catholic flock in Saint Peter's Square for white smoke from the papal chimney.

"I still think she should have invited us," said Dooley.

"What's done is done, Dooley," I said, though I couldn't agree more.

"But why? Why doesn't she want to take us?"

"Because Emerald Rhone is allergic to cats."

Emerald Rhone, the most famous actress of our time, was allergic to cats. It was hard to believe and yet it was true. The moment I heard it, I experienced a slight diminution of my love and timeless admiration for the screen legend.

"I still find it hard to believe Odelia would be invited to

3

spend the weekend with Emerald Rhone," said Dooley. "Does she even know her?"

"I doubt it. As far as I know Odelia's boss wangled the invitation."

Dan Goory, editor of the *Hampton Cove Gazette* and Odelia's boss, prides himself on being the most well-connected man in the Hamptons. His address book is a veritable Who's Who of the rich and famous, and among those luminaries, apparently, is the one and only Emerald, the greatest living actress.

"I can't believe Emerald is allergic to cats," said Dooley.

"I can't believe it either and yet it is so," I said.

We both mused on this most unthinkable thing for a while.

"Now I don't even like her anymore," said Dooley finally. "And I wish I hadn't watched her lousy show."

The show he was referring to was *Big Little Secrets*, which had been a huge ratings hit and had apparently been watched by everyone and their cat. Now that the final episode had aired, the star cast of the show were meeting for the weekend at Emerald's Hamptons home, on the outskirts of Hampton Cove. All five stars were going to be there: Kimberlee Cruz, Verna Rectrix, Abbey Moret, Alina Isman and of course Emerald herself. And Odelia and Chase.

Normally Dan Goory would have gone, as an old friend of Emerald's, but since he had a prior engagement—he was doing a golf tournament in Scotland—he'd decided to send Odelia as his celebrity emissary instead.

Chase suddenly glanced over in our direction. I gulped a little. I know that Chase, Odelia's cop boyfriend, doesn't speak our language, but sometimes I wonder. The man is part of the family, after all, and you never know if Odelia's gift of talking to her cats can be transferred by close association.

"So what do you guys think?" asked Chase now.

"Think about what?" I asked cautiously.

"Is she going to come out of this thing with her sanity intact or should we call off the whole thing?"

"Oh, Marge will fix her right up," said Dooley. "She always does."

Chase gave us a bemused look and chuckled lightly. "You guys are so funny. Do you know that before I met you I never even considered cats as intelligent creatures? I always thought that honor was reserved for dogs."

Both me and Dooley bridled. "Dogs!" I said, stiffening. "Please don't compare us with that foul and horrid breed, Chase. I mean, please!"

"Yeah, dogs are no match for cats," Dooley added.

"No comparison," I agreed. "Like, at all."

Chase had narrowed his eyes at us. "Sometimes I wish I could understand what you're saying. It almost strikes me as meaningful." Then he shook his head. "What am I doing? Talking to a bunch of cats. I must be losing it."

He was losing it, if he was comparing us to dogs. But I decided not to press the point. Chase was obviously under a great deal of stress. He was, after all, Odelia's plus-one for this shindig, and probably just as nervous as she was.

Then again, he didn't look nervous. In fact he looked as cool as a cucumber. A little bored, even. As if he wasn't particularly looking forward to visiting acting royalty as much as Odelia was.

He finally heaved a deep sigh and checked his watch. "If she keeps this up we're going to be late."

Dooley eyed me meaningfully.

"No, Dooley," I said. "We're not going to ask Chase to take us along. For one thing, he doesn't understand what we're saying, and for another, he's a self-declared dog person, and everyone knows dog persons aren't exactly advocates for the rights of cats to join their humans wherever they go."

"Please, Max," he said. "The least we can do is try."

I rolled my eyes. "Oh, all right." So I tapped Chase lightly on the arm.

He looked up. "Mh?"

"Chase," I said, enunciating clearly and deliberately.

"What is it, buddy?" he said, frowning.

This was good news. Maybe he could understand me after all? "Could you please tell Odelia she needs to bring us along on this weekend trip?"

"Yes, please, Chase," said Dooley, giving the burly cop his best puss-in-boots look.

Chase eyed us both curiously for a moment, then laughed. "If I didn't know any better I'd say you guys want to tag along this weekend, don't you?"

"Oh, yes, please!" said Dooley eagerly.

He laughed again. "Fine," he said finally. "I'll take it up with Odelia." He then got up and started pacing the living room floor. "What's taking her so long? She could have packed for a year by now, let alone a weekend."

Dooley and I shared a happy look. Chase was taking up our case.

Which meant we were going on a little trip after all!

# CHAPTER 2

*O*delia had navigated the streets leading out of town deeply lost in thought. It was only when she passed the sign welcoming people to Hampton Cove, the friendliest place in the Hamptons, that she finally realized Chase was talking. She'd been driving on auto-pilot for the past couple of minutes and now looked up. "I'm sorry, what were you saying?"

"I think your cats wanted to tag along," he said, much to her surprise.

"My cats?" She cut him a quick sideways glance. "Did they... tell you that?"

It wasn't possible. Only the women in her family had the gift of being able to talk to cats. Not even her uncle Alec could understand them.

"Yeah, they were putting on a real show while you were upstairs with your mother. Meowing or mewling or mewing or whatever the hell it is that they do." He shook his head. "I gotta tell you, babe. Sometimes those cats of yours could almost pass for humans the way they go on. And the way they look at you! Staring with something akin to actual intelligence in those big eyes."

"Well, cats are highly sensitive and intelligent creatures."

"That, they are. Especially yours." He settled back, stretching out his long legs. "Now are you finally going to relax and enjoy this trip? Ever since Dan asked you to replace him you've been more nervous than a high schooler for their first dance at the prom!"

"I'm sorry," she said. "But this is a big deal. I don't want to let Dan down."

"You're not going to let him down. Just be yourself out there, and everything will be fine."

"You think?"

"Sure. Hey, movie stars are regular people, too, and they're going to be very much themselves this weekend, just a little get-together of friends."

"Yeah—yeah, I guess you're right," she said, even though she had the distinct impression he was wrong. Stars like Emerald Rhone or Alina Isman were never truly themselves when out in public, and that's what this shindig was, after all: a public affair. Otherwise why was she invited? If this was friends and family only, would Emerald have invited Dan? No, this was a public event, and Odelia was going to be subjected to the same scrutiny as the rest of them, which meant she needed to look her absolute and stunning best.

"Besides," Chase went on, "it's not as if we're going to be the center of attention. We'll just be flies on the wall—the guests no one pays attention to."

She nodded, and willed herself to relax her death grip on the steering wheel. Usually Dan handled these high-profile get-togethers. They were important networking opportunities. But more and more he was pushing Odelia to take over for him—introducing her into the world of celebrities.

"With so many famous stars there, we're going to blend

right in," Chase said. "And isn't that the whole point? For you to have access to these people and still be able to write your articles? You're not the star, babe—you just have to mingle with the stars so you can write about them."

She was nodding in agreement. "And that's my strength as a reporter. Not to stand out too much, while at the same time earning the real stars' trust."

"Hey, those stars don't appreciate it if some reporter steals the limelight. So frankly speaking the plainer and less flashy we both look, the better."

She laughed. He was right. Stars hate to be upstaged. She darted a quick look at him. He was looking his usual handsome self. Dressed in tan slacks, aquamarine button-down and penny loafers, he could have featured in a Ralph Lauren ad for menswear. She'd opted for a simple floral-pattern summer dress and still felt underdressed for the occasion. But he was right. They weren't the stars, and they shouldn't try to look like stars, either.

"So about Max and Dooley," she said. "You know I couldn't take them. Dan was very specific about that. No cats allowed."

"I'm sure Emerald would have made an exception. They're housebroken."

"It's not that. Emerald is allergic to cats."

"And yet she's always photographed lugging that little mutt around."

"That's different. A person can be allergic to cats and not to dogs."

"Hey—your cats, your rules, babe."

"And even if Emerald wasn't allergic, it just wouldn't be practical. If I take Max and Dooley, I'd have to take Brutus and Harriet, too, and their bowls and litter boxes, and it would just turn into a whole production and for what? Just so they can spend the weekend at Emerald's? No, they'll be fine with Mom."

She was feeling a little guilty about leaving her cats behind. They were rarely separated for even one night, and now she was going away for a whole weekend. But it was a little impractical, and she could hardly impose on Emerald, who was one of the world's biggest stars. It was a miracle they'd been invited in the first place, so showing up with four cats, their litter boxes, bowls, bags of cat food, favorite blankets, pillows and toys would be nuts.

They'd be fine at her mother's place, who'd make sure they were fed and taken care of. Besides, she was sure the cast of *Big Little Secrets* would all bring their own pets—all dogs—and create trouble for Max and the others.

She wouldn't want Max and the others facing off with a pack of wild Maltipoos, Yorkshire Terriers, Chihuahuas, Shih Tzus or Brussels Griffons!

# CHAPTER 3

That night, the four of us were lying on the couch Marge reserved for us in the family room, while she and her husband Tex and her mother Vesta were watching a movie. It had been Gran's turn to choose the movie, and she had picked one of her favorite ones: *Pearl Harbor*, now playing on the flatscreen.

"I really can't imagine what you see in that movie, Mom," said Marge.

"Shush," said Gran. The big kissing scene between Ben Affleck and Kate Beckinsale was coming up, and she didn't want to miss a thing, as the song goes.

Marge's brother Uncle Alec, a frequent guest, was already half asleep, and Tex looked about to doze off, too. They weren't too big on kissing scenes.

Marge, who'd wanted to watch *The Bachelorette*, didn't look happy either.

"It's flyboys!" said Gran. "How can you not like flyboys?"

"I like flyboys as much as the next fly girl," said Marge, "but what I don't like is watching the same movie over and over and over again."

"It's a classic!" said Gran. "Just like *Titanic*! You never get bored with *Titanic*, do you? So?"

Marge shook her head. This was not an argument she was going to win. "You guys are awfully quiet," she said instead, addressing the four of us.

Reading from left to right there was Dooley, yours truly, Brutus and Harriet. Harriet strictly speaking belongs to Marge, Brutus to Chase, and Dooley to Gran, but basically we consider the entire Poole family our home.

"They're not happy Odelia didn't take them along," said Gran without looking away from her flyboys' exploits. "And quite frankly neither am I."

"Emerald is allergic to cats. Some people are," said Marge.

"You mean to tell me that Emerald Rhone, reigning queen of Tinseltown, is allergic to cats? I don't believe it."

"That's what Odelia told me."

Gran was shaking her head and muttering something under her breath. She wasn't a big fan of people who weren't big fans of cats.

"She can't help it if she's allergic, can she?" said Marge. "It's a medical thing."

"Medical thing my ass. I'll bet she's faking it."

"That's crazy. Why would she fake being allergic to cats?"

"For the attention! These Hollywood types all have imaginary medical conditions. I'll bet she's not allergic to cats at all, just making a big thing out of it. And meanwhile poor Max is deprived the company of his favorite human."

"I like to think we're all Max's favorite humans," said Marge a little huffily.

"Cats like Max attach themselves to one human for life, and in his case that human happens to be Odelia—so tough luck for the rest of us."

"Well," said Marge. "I'm sure you're just imagining it. Max loves all of us exactly the same. Isn't that right, Max?"

To be honest I wasn't in the mood to put Marge's mind at ease that I liked her very much, too, thank you very much. Gran was right. I missed my human. Yeah, I know what you're all thinking: cats don't miss their humans. Cats are independent creatures and they don't care if their human lives or dies and yadda yadda yadda. Well, let me tell you that's all fake news, people. Cats get attached to their humans just as much as the next canine, or at least this particular feline does. And I was just wondering what Odelia was doing at that moment when Marge's phone sang out the theme song from the reboot of *Beverly Hills, 90210.*

"Hey, honey, have you settled in all right?" she asked.

"Ask her about the sheets," said Gran, nudging her daughter. "And ask her about the food. Oh, and ask her if it's true that Emerald's skin looks like a drumhead from all those facelifts and those gallons and gallons of Botox."

"Have you met Emerald yet?" asked Marge, ignoring her mother. "You have? Ooh, how exciting! So what is she like? Is she nice?"

And while the adults in the room prattled on, and Ben Affleck was fighting the good fight over in Europe while his best friend was hitting on his girl, I noticed for the first time that my compadres were all very quiet indeed.

"Is everything all right?" I asked, giving Brutus a slight nudge.

"Oh, Max," was his response. It didn't sound like he was all right at all.

I cut a glance to Harriet, who merely rolled her expressive eyes at me.

"What's going on with him?" I mouthed.

"Don't ask!" she mouthed back.

"What's going on with Brutus, Max?" asked Dooley now.

"I don't know. I asked him and he wouldn't say."

"Ask him if it's menopause," said Dooley.

"Menopause is a human thing, Dooley."

"Oh?"

"It's not menopause," said Harriet. "It's worse—much worse."

"Worse?" asked Dooley. "What could be worse than menopause?"

"Like I said, menopause is a human thing and doesn't—"

"Cancer!" said Dooley suddenly. "Do you have cancer, Brutus?"

Dooley has a tendency to think that whenever someone doesn't feel A-Okay, it's because they are suffering from cancer. Or, apparently, menopause.

"No, it's not cancer," said Brutus gruffly. "Though sometimes I wish it was."

That sounded ominous. And now, of course, I was more curious than ever.

"He misses Odelia," said Dooley knowingly. He patted Brutus on the paw. "Don't worry, buddy," he said loudly. "She'll be back before you know it!"

Brutus merely grumbled something. It didn't sound overly friendly.

So it wasn't Odelia either. So what could it be?

"I know!" said Dooley. "Of course! How silly of me. You miss Chase, don't you?" He patted the butch black cat on the paw again. "Don't worry, buddy. Chase will be back before you know it. And I'm sure he misses you too."

"I don't miss Chase, and will you stop touching me!"

"Touchy," Dooley muttered.

"If you have to know…" Harriet began.

"Don't you dare," growled Brutus.

"They're your friends, Brutus. They have a right to know."

"No, they don't!"

"Brutus is having trouble with—"

"Stop talking now!"

"His inner male," Harriet finally finished.

Dooley and I stared at the big cat. Whatever I'd expected, it wasn't this.

"I'm sorry, what did you say?" I asked.

"Brutus feels that maybe he's a female trapped in a male's body, and now he's thinking about talking to someone."

I stared from Brutus to Harriet and back. "I don't get it," I said.

"Me neither," said Dooley. "Who's inside Brutus's body talking to him?"

"Nobody!" Brutus exploded. "It's just that... have you never wondered if you were who you thought you were or maybe you were really someone else?"

I blinked. "Um, you lost me there," I said.

"Me, too," said Dooley.

"I mean, society has all these expectations of a male cat. Just look at me. I'm butch, I'm handsome, I'm strong—your stereotypical hard-nosed male, right?"

"Uh-huh," I said. "Go on."

"Well, what if deep down I'm a tender-hearted, sweet-natured... female?!"

Dooley and I shared a look, then burst into a hearty bout of laughter.

"I knew it!" cried Brutus, and jumped down from the couch. "I knew you two wouldn't understand!" And off he went, slinking away with a panther-like grace—or was it a pantheress?

"Wait, he's not kidding?" I said.

"Nuh-uh," said Harriet. "And the worst part is, now he's trying to convince me that maybe deep down I'm a male, and not a female as I always thought."

"But you *are* a female," I said.

"Duh," she said.

"You're probably the most female feline of all the female felines around," said Dooley deferentially.

She permitted herself a slight smile. "Thanks, Dooley. That's very sweet of you to say."

I was still reeling. "So when did Brutus…"

"Figure he might be a female trapped in a male body? After he saw a documentary on the subject," said Harriet. "It's gotten him all confused. And the worst part? He's lost all interest in me!"

"That *is* bad," Dooley agreed, though he didn't sound sorry. Dooley has always had a crush on Harriet, and I had the distinct impression he wouldn't mind Brutus turning into a female so he could take his place by Harriet's side.

And we would probably have explored the topic a lot further, if not suddenly Marge thrust her phone to my ear and I heard the most beautiful sound in the world: the voice of my human asking me how I was holding up.

# CHAPTER 4

"Oh, I'm fine," I said breezily.

"I'm sorry I didn't take you, Max, but—"

"Emerald is allergic to cats. I know. You told me."

"And you know how it is with these superstars—it's their way or the highway."

"So how is the house? Plenty of nooks and crannies where a cat can get lost, I reckon?"

"Oh, Max, this must be the biggest house I've ever seen."

"Is it true Emerald pampers her dog as if it's her baby?"

Odelia laughed. "Oh, yeah. I haven't talked to Emerald yet, apart from meeting her when we arrived, but she was holding the famous Fanny in her arms the entire time. She really adores her."

"So she's a Maltipoo, right?"

"No, a teacup Pomsky."

"Why is it that there are a million different kinds of dogs but only one kind of cat? Probably because dogs like to show off, huh?"

"I got to run, Max. I just heard the dinner gong."

"Dinner gong? Emerald has an actual dinner gong?"

"Talk to you soon, Maxie. Give Dooley and the others a big kiss."

And before I could tell her nighty-night, she was gone.

I heaved a deep sigh.

"Don't worry, Maxie," said Marge. "She'll be back before you know it."

Why did everybody keep saying Odelia would be back before I knew it? I knew she was gone now, and that was what counted. And before you think I'm one of those pampered pets the superstars of this world like so much, I'm not, okay. But I like to sleep on my own couch, prance around my own kitchen, and visit any of a number of favorite spots—and since Marge had locked up Odelia's house for the time being, and transferred my food bowl, water bowl and litter box to hers, it wasn't the same. Then again, it was only for a couple of days, and then things would all go back to normal again.

So I decided to stop whining and accept my fate. I mean, how often can you watch *Pearl Harbor* in the company of your friends and family? If you're like Gran, probably a million times. So I put my head down, and dozed off.

🐾

"Who was that?" asked Chase as Odelia put her phone away.

"My mom," said Odelia.

"She misses you, huh?"

"Yeah, well, you know how she is. She worries about me."

Chase smiled and pulled her into a hug. "That's so sweet. My mom probably doesn't even remember my name."

She hugged him close. Chase's mom was living with her sister now, after her memory started failing her. Sometimes she remembered she had a son, other times she didn't. So

Odelia counted her blessings, and was glad everyone at home was fine, cats included.

"So," said Chase when the dinner bell rang out a second time. "I guess that's us."

"That's us and that's dinner," said Odelia. "At least I think it is."

"Could be the fire alarm, but I don't think so."

Odelia had put her suitcase on the bed and had been in the process of unpacking but that would have to wait until later. First dinner, and hopefully meeting some of the people that had arrived after they had. In fact she couldn't wait to meet them all. Emerald had been part of the welcoming committee, along with her husband Pete, but they hadn't seen the others yet.

"So how do I look?" asked Chase as he paraded in front of her.

She lifted an eyebrow. "I thought you didn't care what people thought of you?"

"Well, I care a little," he said with a grin.

He'd donned an ivory dinner jacket, blue twill shirt with invisible stripe, purple tie with little pink fishes and his best chestnut brogues.

"You look very Hollywood," she said.

He struck a pose. "Hey. That's what we're all here for."

She studied herself in the mirror. She'd decided to wear her little black dress with her favorite black pumps. When in doubt, black never fails.

"How about me?" she asked as she twirled around.

"In a word: stunning," he said as he studied her with abject admiration.

"Don't you think I overdid it on the mascara?"

"Honey, there's no such thing as too much mascara."

"You don't know what mascara is, do you?"

"Not a clue."

She gave him a quick peck on the cheek. "You're adorable."

She clutched her faux Louis Vuitton clutch under her arm, and headed for the door, but Chase blocked her with a wolfish grin. "We still have time."

She laughed a throaty laugh, placed a finger on his chest and pushed. "Later, gator. Wouldn't want to be late for Emerald's dinner party, would we?"

"How about a little late?" he said huskily.

She tsk-tsked gently and whispered, "Later you can take all of this…" She gestured to the little black dress. "… off."

"Can't wait," he growled.

The moment they walked out into the hall, doors to the left and right of them disgorged more participants for Emerald's weekend getaway. To her left, Odelia recognized the gorgeous Kimberlee Cruz and a young man with a buzz cut who presumably was her boyfriend. To the right the always elegant Alina Isman emerged from her room, a swish in her step and a regal expression on her face, accompanied by the famous Reinhart Bergé, the rock star.

Oh, boy, Odelia thought, before taking a deep breath, plastering her best smile onto her face, and greeting first Alina and then Kimberlee. Introductions were exchanged, and the men flocked together while the women did the same.

"So a reporter, huh?" said Alina. "I thought Emerald outlawed reporters?"

"She made an exception for my boss, who's an old friend," Odelia explained. "But then he couldn't make it so he sent me —with Emerald's permission, of course."

"I just hope you won't write all kinds of saucy things about us when we're drunk in the sauna and making fools of ourselves," said the fifty-something actress with a kittenish laugh.

Alina looked stunning, as usual: her alabaster skin, accentuated by bright red lipstick, and those amazing piercing green eyes. Her long reddish hair framed her face and her slender form was clad in a green chiffon designer dress. In spite of her age, the woman was simply… glowing.

Kimberlee, the youngest, likewise looked amazing. She was a round-faced young woman, only twenty-five, but with the acting chops of a much older person, courtesy of her early start in the business. She was the rising star and had been dubbed the new Emerald—a fact that hadn't escaped the real Emerald's attention, who'd even gone so far as to practically hand her crown to Kimberlee in a double inter-view for *Vanity Fair* last year.

"I think it's great that you're here," said Kimberlee in her trademark raspy voice. "Give us a sense of reality. It's so easy to get lost in Emerald's world, as she's such a superstar, and a reporter present will keep us all from doing silly things like fawn over Queen Emerald and lie at her feet." She laughed.

"And give away all of our deepest, darkest secrets," Alina added.

"Frankly I don't worry about that," said Kimberlee. "At this point I feel I've got nothing to hide—I've spilled all of my secrets, deep, dark and otherwise."

"Oh, have you now," said Alina, giving her colleague a knowing look.

Kimberlee laughed. "Well, maybe not *all* of my secrets. A girl has to keep a few up her sleeve, right? Keep the mystery?"

Odelia wondered what those secrets could be. But then she reminded herself she wasn't here as a representative of the *National Enquirer* or *Star*.

They descended a sweeping marble staircase, Alina's finely manicured fingers lightly touching the gilt balustrade. On the wall, a life-size portrait of Emerald hung, posing on a throne as if she were the Queen of England.

"Oh, now will you look at that!" Alina exclaimed.

"That wasn't there last year, was it?" said Kimberlee.

"The Queen of Hollywood. A little presumptuous, don't you think?"

"Well, she is the Queen, isn't she?"

"Or was."

Both women laughed at some joke Odelia wasn't privy to.

"Don't mind us," said Alina quickly, hooking her arm in Odelia's. "We're just making fun."

"Of Emerald?" asked Odelia.

She caught the warning look Kimberlee shot Alina and the latter, who'd clearly been dipping into the preprandial martinis, zipped up her lips and mimicked throwing away the key.

Maybe she shouldn't have announced the fact that she was a reporter, Odelia thought now. People tended to clam up when they knew. Then again, Emerald would have told everyone anyway, so there was no point in hiding.

Downstairs, a liveried servant escorted the small company into the dining room, and Odelia's breath momentarily caught as she was struck by the sheer opulence. Three crystal chandeliers lit up the room. Gilt sconces illuminated paintings of old masters adorning the walls, and the floor was exquisite marble. A glass of champagne was discreetly pressed into her hand and she and Chase were equally discreetly led to the table by another servant.

She recognized Abbey Moret, who was loudly regaling Verna Rectrix and Verna's husband Thaw Roman with some anecdote, making the couple laugh, and as Odelia glanced around, eyes shining, she saw that all the guests were there except for Emerald and her husband Pete.

"I'll bet she'll be the last one to arrive," said Chase, as if he'd read her mind.

"She is, after all, the Queen of Hollywood," said Odelia. "Did you have a chance to chat with Alina's husband?"

"Yeah, actually I did. He seems like a good guy. Said something about his wife having suffered a migraine this afternoon and almost deciding not to come down for dinner."

"She didn't look like she was suffering from a headache."

"The magic of Ibuprofen, no doubt. Reinhart said she suffers migraines so frequently she carries a small pharmacy wherever she goes."

"And here I thought she was tipsy."

Next to them, Kimberlee's boyfriend was taking a selfie with his girlfriend. He looked as impressed with the setup as they were.

"His name is Zoltan Falecki," said Chase, following Odelia's gaze. "He's a hockey player and a pretty great guy. First-time invitee to this famous bash."

"This is a famous bash?"

"Apparently it is. Every time Emerald wraps a project, she invites the main cast to her house. A way for her to stay in touch with her co-stars. Get to know them a little better."

"And to assert her superiority," said Odelia.

Chase grinned. "You said it."

The moment had come: the lights in the room were dimmed, and suddenly there she was: the queen herself. Emerald Rhone, resplendent in a long black gown with plunging neckline, a diamond necklace adding even more luster.

"Oh. My. God," murmured Chase, and Odelia couldn't have put it better.

# CHAPTER 5

"*M*y beloved friends!" Emerald said, as her diamonds shimmered intoxicatingly. "Welcome to my humble abode!"

Loud cheers rang out around the table, and Odelia had the distinct impression this was a ritual many of those present had gone through before. Then she remembered this was the second season of *Big Little Secrets* that had been broadcast, so these same people had been here before, exactly one year ago, presumably without any media people present.

"My darlings," said Emerald with a smile on her face as she glanced around the room. She spread her arms to encompass all those present. "I'm happy—so happy to see all of your lovely faces here tonight. This business of ours can be cutthroat sometimes, and it's moments like these that remind us all that in spite of that, friendships do exist and thrive—only if we let them!"

"Hear hear," said Abbey, raising her glass and taking a sip.

"I invited you all here because I admire you—powerful ladies—beautiful ladies—gorgeous creatures!"

Loud laughs and whoops around the room, then Emerald gestured for silence.

"But most importantly because I love you all." She raised her own glass. "May you prosper and be happy beyond compare. And know that you'll always have a staunch friend and ambassador in me—salut!"

"Salut!" Alina shouted, and all glasses were now raised.

"Oh, and before I forget!" Emerald said, "I wanted to give a shout-out to one person in particular." She cast a loving glance in Kimberlee Cruz's direction. "Kimberlee." She laughed. "My sweet, darling Kimberlee. How you have grown —how you have blossomed—how you have turned into ... me!"

Laughs around the room at this, though not from Kimberlee, who seemed stunned at so much praise. Her hand clutching her chest, she stared at Emerald with a mixture of surprise and adoration.

"This year marks my fiftieth year in show business—my fiftieth year! I'll be seventy next month, and someone told me —oh, where is he... my rock, my support? My..." She gestured with her glass to her husband Pete. "Pete reminded me that it is customary in the private sector to retire at sixty-five, and by those standards I'm long overdue! In all seriousness, though, his words hit home. I am long past my prime— no, no," she said, raising a hand when the group protested. "It's true. Of course there are those who say that, like a fine wine, actors get better with age. I'm not so sure about that!" She raised her glass again. "If there's anyone I see as my successor it's you, my beloved Kimberlee. Here's to many wonderful years in the business. Salut, my sweet."

Kimberlee, who'd gasped at these words, murmured her thanks.

Odelia wondered whether any of this was real, or just for show. She did have the impression that the other women were not too pleased by this surprise endorsement of Kimberlee as the successor to the reigning queen of Hollywood. Alina, in particular, seemed utterly shocked, if her expression was anything to go by, and was whispering furiously to her husband.

Abbey had an enigmatic smile plastered on her face, which could well be hiding her own displeasure at Emerald's words. And Verna looked positively disgusted. The diminutive woman had been dipping into her glass long before the first toast, and now said something to her husband Thaw. When there was a sudden lull in the conversation she could very clearly be heard saying, "Bastard!" before being induced by Thaw to take a seat and slapping his hand away when he tried to relieve her of her glass of champagne.

"I have a feeling all is not well in paradise," said Chase as they took their own seats.

"I have the same impression," said Odelia. She knew Thaw Roman was also an actor, though not a very famous one, and he looked very unhappy to be there right now. Though maybe that was his default expression.

Emerald sat at the head of the table, Pete at her side, while Alina sat closest, with Kimberlee on her right. Verna and Abbey sat furthest away, with Odelia and Chase sitting at the other end of the long table. A man Odelia didn't recognize sat at the other end.

"Who's he?" asked Chase now.

"No idea. He doesn't look familiar."

Abbey, who was at Odelia's elbow, and had heard the question, leaned in and said, "That's Odo Hardy. He's the director. He's German and a genius."

A blond pixyish woman in her early forties, Odelia couldn't help but marvel at the texture of Abbey's skin. It looked like velvet, with no visible pores whatsoever, contrary to most women her age. She made a mental note to ask her about her skincare secrets if she got the chance.

"So you're the reporter, right?" asked Abbey cheerfully as she placed her napkin across her lap. She was wearing a strapless yellow dress revealing quite a bit of cleavage and looked like Cinderella at the ball.

"Yup. That's me," said Odelia. "I'm the reporter."

"Cool," said Abbey with a smile, and Odelia liked her already.

"Can I just say I'm a great admirer of your work, Miss Moret? I think I have seen every single one of your movies."

"Ah, that's so sweet of you," Abbey said, without much conviction. She took another swig from her glass and gave the cutest little burp. "Oopsie."

"So what did you make of Emerald's speech?" asked Odelia.

"Mh? Oh, that." Abbey shrugged. "Very noble of her, I thought, to appoint a successor. Of course, if I were younger she might have picked me. Not that Kimberlee doesn't deserve the praise. She is, after all, an amazing actress. An amazing talent—simply amazing." She darted a quick look at Kimberlee that didn't seem overly friendly, then directed a sweet smile at Odelia. "I'm sorry, but what did you say your name was again?"

"Odelia Poole. And this is my boyfriend, Chase Kingsley."

"Chase." Abbey gave Chase an appraising look. "Are you an actor, Chase? You look like an actor."

"I'm a cop, actually, Miss Moret," said Chase.

"A cop!" Abbey's eyes went a little dreamy. "Oh, my. Are you here to make an arrest, Officer Kingsley? Or to perform a strip search, perhaps?"

Chase laughed. "I'm simply here as Odelia's plus-one, I'm afraid."

"Oh, so you're not here in an official capacity, huh? Too

bad. Too bad. The evening could have used some excitement. Oh, well. I guess we'll have to muddle through somehow." She took another swig from her drink, until her husband took her glass away with a censorious look. "Oopsie," Abbey repeated, but this time with a nasty scowl directed at her hubby. She made a grab for her glass but he kept it out of reach.

"Don't you think you've had enough for one night?"

"No, I don't," she said.

"Well, I think you have."

Abbey leaned closer. "That's my husband Seger. He says he's a talent agent but his job title is actually Party Pooper. And he's very good at what he does." When Seger grunted something, she added, "Yep, he's a party-pooping talent agent. Or a talented party pooper. Not sure which." She giggled.

Her husband held out his hand. "Seger Glik. So nice to meet you."

Odelia shook it, and so did Chase.

"Don't mind my wife," he said. "She's pretty excitable. Which is what we all love about her."

"Ooh, thank you, munchkin," she said, and gave him an exaggerated kiss. Turning back to Odelia, she said, "One thing I'll say for Emerald. She knows how to throw a good party. Have you been to one of these things before?"

"No, I can't say that I have," said Odelia.

"Oh, you're gonna love it. She has the best chef in the world, and I mean, that man can cook!"

"I'll vouch for that," said Seger. "Expect to gain a couple pounds."

Suddenly there was a commotion on the other side of the table. Verna Rectrix had risen to her feet and was loudly proclaiming, "Don't tell me what to do, you bastard!"

Her husband, to whom these words were apparently

directed, looked appropriately embarrassed. "Darling, please —you're making a scene."

"Of course I'm making a scene!" cried Verna. "And if you don't like it you shouldn't have married an actress!" At this, she threw a vicious look at Kimberlee, who was sitting next to her. "And as for you—you hussy!" she screamed, then threw the contents of her glass at Kimberlee's chest.

Kimberlee gasped in shock, then her face flushed and her eyes shot fire. And she would have accosted Verna if not her own boyfriend and Verna's husband had interfered, and held the two women apart.

"What's going on there?" asked Odelia.

"Oh, that's just Verna being Verna. I'm not sure if you can tell but she has quite the temper. She used to pull these stunts on set all the time."

Verna stomped off, shouting something Odelia didn't quite catch.

"Oops, looks like someone is going to miss dinner," commented Abbey. "Well, no matter—it's not as if she'd eat it. She's like a stick insect as it is."

"She is very slender," Odelia agreed.

"Slender?" scoffed Abbey. "More like one of those models who can't stop puking up their food." She leaned in. "Shall I let you in on a little secret?"

Odelia nodded. "Sure."

"The secret of staying skinny. Cocaine. Lots of cocaine. Just ask Verna."

Odelia blinked, and wondered if Abbey would be telling her these things if she hadn't just downed three glasses of champagne in quick succession.

"Oh, my," she said.

"You stick with me, kid. I'll teach you a thing or two about Hollywood's elite."

"Abbey!" hissed her husband.

"What?" said Abbey innocently.

"Shut up! She's a reporter!"

Abbey fixed her unsteady gaze on Odelia. "She don't look like a reporter to me."

"Well, I am, actually," said Odelia, feeling she should probably give Abbey another warning that everything she said could and would be used against her in an article of reporting.

Abbey grinned a little luridly. "I don't care! You hear me? I don't care! I simply don't care!" She then clasped an arm around Odelia's shoulders and gave her a smacking kiss on the cheek. "I like you anyway, you fair-haired little minx. Reporter or no reporter—I'm not going to hold it against you." She slammed the table hard. "What does a person have to do to get some food around here?!"

Oh, boy, thought Odelia. This was shaping up to be a very interesting weekend indeed.

# CHAPTER 6

*N*ight had fallen, and the house was quiet. *Pearl Harbor* had finally finished, with Gran happy that Ben Affleck's girl had found love again in the arms of Josh Hartnett, and the humans had all retired to bed. I was sitting outside on the porch swing, Dooley next to me, with Brutus and Harriet out and about somewhere, and both of us wondering what Odelia was doing right then.

"I think she's missing us so much she'll probably be back in the morning," said Dooley.

"Don't count on it," I said. "Odelia is probably having the time of her life."

"Oh, don't say that, Max. She's probably miserable is what I think."

"Humans are different from cats, Dooley," I told him. "They don't miss us the way we miss them. It's more a case of out of sight out of mind for them."

"You really think so?" He looked both surprised and disappointed.

"Oh, sure. In fact she probably has her eye on another pet already. If what she told us was true, that Emerald Rhone person has a house full of pets, and she probably hands them out like candy to her guests. It wouldn't surprise me if Odelia arrives home with a whole brood of new pets in tow."

"But, Max, that's terrible!"

"It is," I agreed, placing my head on my paws and staring moodily into the night.

"What you need is something to distract you," said Dooley, giving me a poke.

I merely grunted something. I was in no mood to do distracting things.

"Come on. Let' s go and see what Brutus and Harriet are up to."

"Hanky-panky, probably," I said morosely.

"Or at least let's go to cat choir. This is the one night you need to be surrounded by other cats, Max. It will keep you from thinking bad thoughts."

"I'm not thinking bad thoughts—I'm thinking realistic thoughts—really getting down and dirty on what life as Odelia's cat is all about."

"Oh, Max, don't be this way," said Dooley. "This isn't you. You're usually the sane and sensible one, and I'm the one whining and complaining and getting all worked up about stuff."

In spite of my foul mood, I had to laugh at this rare moment of self-reflection on my best friend's part. "You're right about that," I said.

"See? You're smiling already! All you need is to have your friends around, and you'll soon forget all about Odelia and those fun and interesting pets she's having a good time with right now."

And there he'd spoiled the moment again, and I sunk back into my slough of despond.

For a moment, we just sat there, thinking about what could have been, and then another fun and interesting pet came slinking up to the porch, mounted it with some effort, and climbed the swing.

"Brutus," I muttered.

"Max, Dooley," muttered Brutus.

"Brutus," muttered Dooley.

For a moment, no one spoke, me thinking dark thoughts about Odelia and the fickleness of human affection, Dooley thinking dark thoughts about me and the fickleness of my mood, and Brutus... Oh, who cared what Brutus was thinking about?

Then, finally, Dooley broke the silence. "So where is Harriet? I thought you were going to do some hanky-panky—what is hanky-panky, by the way, Max? You never said."

"Hanky-panky is a, um, fun game," I said, in spite of my foul mood still very serious at protecting Dooley's innocence.

"What kind of game?" he said, perking up. "Can we play it?"

"Not right now," I said after a pause. "Besides, it's a game usually played between a tomcat and a queen."

"So can I play it with Harriet?"

"Theoretically, you could," I agreed, darting a glance in Brutus's direction. Usually these were fighting words. Now he just lay there, like a sack of potatoes.

"Brutus?" I asked. "Are you all right, buddy?"

Brutus merely grunted something that gave me the impression he was far from all right.

"What was that? I didn't quite catch it."

"I said, rotten. And now will you please let me wallow in self-loathing in peace and quiet. Self-loathing requires that everyone around keeps their traps shut."

So Dooley and I kept our traps shut for a moment. Then, because it's hard to keep a good cat quiet, Dooley said, "So when you see Harriet could you ask her if she wants to play hanky-panky with me?"

Brutus directed a look of such hostility at Dooley that even the latter, though usually not the quickest on the uptake, got it amidships and gulped.

"Harriet is upset with me right now," said Brutus finally. "So if you don't mind I'm not going to ask her anything. She'd only cut me if I did."

"Upset with you?" I asked, deciding to take the risk of digging a little deeper into this mysterious matter. "And why is that?"

"Probably because you didn't let her win at hanky-panky," said Dooley. "Harriet hates losing. You should know this by now, Brutus. Always let her win at everything. It's the only way to keep the peace."

"Oh, shut up, Dooley," said Brutus.

Dooley shut up, and so did I. From vast experience I knew that when Brutus was brooding on something the truth would come out sooner or later. It's not easy keeping stuff bottled up, especially when surrounded by two cats who very much like to know. And clearly I was right, for he suddenly muttered, "Just because I asked her to get in touch with her inner male she has to go and fly off the handle like that."

"You asked Harriet to get in touch with her inner male?" I asked, stifling a sudden urge to giggle.

He stared at me for a moment, daring me to laugh, but I managed to keep up my poker face pretty well.

"Now why would you go and do a thing like that?" asked Dooley.

"Because we're a couple, and if I'm going to get in touch with my inner female, it only makes sense that she gets in touch with her inner male! So we can.... you know... the switcheroo thing."

We both stared at him. Now I was at a complete and utter loss. "Switcheroo thing?" I finally asked.

"Yeah, like in the documentary. The male of the species turns into the female of the species and the female of the species into the male and they live happily ever after. It's not rocket science, you guys."

It sounded like rocket science to me. "So you want to turn into a female and for Harriet to turn into a male so you can live happily ever after?" I asked, wanting to make sure I got the gist of the thing before we proceeded into the nitty-gritty.

"Yeah. We are a couple, after all, and if I'm going to be the female, she has to be the male, right?"

"Um... you could always turn into a female while Harriet keeps on being a female, too," suggested Dooley.

Brutus frowned. "I don't get it."

"Well, if Harriet doesn't want to be a male, and you are adamant about being a female, you're going to be two females together, right?"

"Okay," said Brutus. Then the profundity of Dooley's words settled in and his frown deepened. "I guess... that could work."

"Of course it could work!" I said. "Humans do it all the time. Males with other males, females with other females. It's a very common thing."

"Huh," said Brutus as he tried to wrap his head around it. "The thing is... how are we going to have babies?"

"You adopt," I said knowingly. I'd seen a few Discovery Channel documentaries myself, and more than a few National Geographic ones, too.

"Adopt," said Brutus dubiously. "Why would we adopt when I have a perfectly functioning... you-know-what?"

"If you're going to turn into a female they're going to cut

off your perfectly functioning you-know-what, Brutus," I explained.

Brutus's eyes widened to their maximum dilation. "Wait, what?!"

"What?!" Dooley cried, a few seconds later. His penny usually took a little longer to drop.

"Of course! How can you be a fully functioning female with a fully functioning male you-know-what? That doesn't make sense."

Brutus directed a slightly panicky look at me. "Oh, Max. This is all so very, very complicated!"

"That's why humans visit shrinks to sort through this kind of stuff." And since I'm not a fully functioning shrink, I thought maybe Brutus should see an official one instead of gabbing to his friends about this most important topic.

"You should see a shrink," finally said Dooley, who'd come to the same conclusion I had.

"A shrink? But I don't want to see a shrink!"

"You have to," I said. "You're obviously confused about this issue, Brutus, and the sooner you work through it the sooner you'll be a fully functioning boyfriend—or girlfriend —again."

"Oh, man," he said, shaking his head. "I'm screwed, aren't I?"

"At least one of us is," suddenly a familiar voice rang out in the night. It was Harriet, and she did not look happy.

"We were just telling Brutus he needs to see a shrink," I said.

"I don't know who he should see, but he better make it quick, cause I'm losing patience with this ridiculous cat," said Harriet.

"Do we even know a shrink?" asked Dooley.

I thought hard. None of my acquaintances had studied shrinkage, as far as I knew. Then again, it's not as if cats actually go to school or even college. I guess we're all students of the school of life.

"Kingman might know a shrink," I said. "He's usually well-informed."

Kingman is the cat that belongs to the owner of Hampton Cove's general store. He knows pretty much anyone who's anyone and a whole bunch of absolute nobodies, too.

"Come on," I said, jumping down from the swing. "Let's go see him now."

"Max!" said Dooley. "You're back!"

"Hey," I said, surprised. "I am!" He was right. I was feeling a lot better.

"See," said Dooley. "All you needed was something to take your mind off your human abandoning you and falling in love with a bunch of other, better and nicer pets than you."

Ugh. Whatever Dooley was, it definitely was not a shrink.

More like an anti-shrink.

# CHAPTER 7

*D*inner was over, and what a glorious dinner it was! Emerald's chef had gone all-out preparing the small company the most delicious meal imaginable.

Pork Wellington with prosciutto and spinach-mushroom stuffing. Peppery greens with Meyer-lemon dressing. Rutabaga-sweet potato mash with garlic and sage. And for dessert no-bake chocolate-eggnog crème brûlée. Because in Emerald's view, why limit eggnog to Christmas when you can enjoy it year-round!

The company had retired to the terrace, chatting away and enjoying some of the best wines from Emerald's obviously extensive wine collection.

The house was located near the ocean, and Abbey had already suggested they go for a midnight swim, but since everyone was still too full after the sumptuous meal, her suggestion had fallen on deaf ears.

Candles had been lit, music drifted from hidden speakers, and a gazebo provided privacy for the guests who needed it. Verna had returned—apparently hunger had vanquished whatever rancor she'd been harboring—and was now quietly chatting away with her husband, clutching a glass of wine in one hand and a giant reefer in the other.

Odelia studied the house, which was lit up and looked like a fairytale castle out of a Disney movie.

"Amazing, isn't it?" she said. She was feeling mellow.

"Yeah, it's a nice little hovel," Chase agreed.

"Hovel? It's like a Snow White's castle or something."

Chase laughed. "So who's Snow White and who's the evil stepmother?"

They glanced around. Emerald sat holding court: her director, husband and Alina and Alina's husband at her feet, hanging on her every word. Kimberlee, oddly enough, wasn't amongst those fawning fans, even though she'd been officially named Emerald's successor.

"I'm not sure," said Odelia. "Emerald seems like a shoo-in for Snow White but somehow I don't see her as the young and beautiful bride-to-be."

"Kimberlee, maybe? She's young and pretty. Has the world at her feet."

Odelia poked Chase's nose. She was a little tipsy. "Calling Kimberlee young and pretty, huh?"

"My apologies. You are obviously the only one worthy of Snow White's crown."

"In which case the evil stepmother would be Abbey's husband Seger, who seems to think since I'm a reporter no one should be allowed to talk to me."

"You have to admit it is a little tricky for celebs to talk to reporters."

"I'm not that kind of reporter," she said, slurring her words a little. "I would never take words out of context and put them in someone else's, um…"

"Mouth," he finished, and took her glass away from her. "I have the impression you've had enough for one night, Snow

White. What will the seven dwarfs think when you stomp all over their little beds?"

"I'll lie on their beds, eat their food and even, oh, dear, sit on their little chairs and possibly break them," she said. She patted his face. "So if you're Prince Charming, what are you waiting for to kiss me, handsome?"

A loud cackling sound could be heard. It came from Alina, who had thrown her head back and was laughing with such fakeness Odelia wondered if she was the only one to notice.

"Another fine candidate for evil stepmother," said Chase.

"She would be a perfect evil stepmother," Odelia admitted. "So if she offers us an apple, let's say no."

"Say no to apples. Sounds like a good idea," Chase agreed.

A man joined them, looking slightly worse for wear. "So you're the reporter, eh?" he said, studying Odelia as if trying to determine if she was rabid or not.

"I am, but I don't bite," she assured him.

He laughed. "I'm not so sure about that. So who do you work for? *Variety? The Hollywood Reporter? Deadline Hollywood?*"

"The *Hampton Cove Gazette.*"

He frowned. "*Hampton Cove Gazette?* Never heard of it."

"It's the local rag."

"Local rag?" He looked appropriately confused. "Weird."

"Are you saying I am weird?" asked Odelia with a frown.

"No, the fact that you're here is weird," said the guy, who Odelia now recognized as Kimberlee Cruz's boyfriend, the hockey player. "The only reason I can think of for Emerald to invite you is that she wanted her big announcement to be spread outside of this small company."

"What big announcement?" Odelia asked, wondering if she'd missed a crucial part of the evening.

"You were there. Emerald announced that she's abdicating her throne and crowning Kimberlee as her official successor."

"Oh, yeah, I heard that. I thought that was just a Hollywood thing. Like, just some silly babble?"

"Oh, no," said the guy.

With his buzz cut he reminded her of Chris Evans. For a hockey player he was definitely handsome. Movie-star handsome, in fact.

"So no silly babble?" asked Chase.

"Absolutely not. This is big. Like, career-defining big. In fact Emerald said those exact same words before dinner. Said she was going to make a big announcement. We had no idea she was going to do this—and in front of a member of the press, too." He gestured with his glass to Odelia. "So you better quote me as saying that Kimberlee is honored and extremely pleased. She also wants it to be known that of course there's no way she'll ever be able to follow in the footsteps of a woman as accomplished, as legendary and universally beloved as Emerald Rhone, without a doubt the greatest actress that has ever lived. But she accepts it as a compliment and hopes to do her proud."

"Um, thanks," said Odelia, a little uncertain about this whole spiel.

"So what do you really think?" asked Chase now. "I mean, off the record."

Zoltan stared at Odelia's hands for a moment, as if expecting her to switch off her tape recorder and announce this was really off the record.

"Off the record I think the woman is completely off her rocker," he said finally, relaxing now that he wasn't on an official mission from his girlfriend to butter up the press. "I mean, who cares what Emerald frickin' Rhone thinks? As if she gets to decide who's successful in this business or not. Hollywood is not a kingdom and she's not its queen. There's no throne to give away and no crown to be handed over. Everything Kim has achieved she's done by working harder than anyone out there, and she definitely doesn't need some has-been lush to crown her the next queen of Hollywood."

"Harsh words," said Chase.

"Off the record, though, right?" said Zoltan, suddenly nervous.

"Absolutely," said Odelia. She just hoped she'd remember half of what the guy was saying and vowed to jot it all down in her little notebook the moment they got back to their room.

"Emerald is yesterday's news," Zoltan continued. "Ask around. Everybody thinks so. The only reason we decided to humor her and accept her invitation was because of Abbey and Alina. Kim respects them tremendously. If not for those two she would have turned Emerald down flat. Especially after what she did to her."

"What did she do to her?"

Zoltan leaned a little closer and lowered his voice. "She tried to get Kimberlee kicked off the show. Said she was only going to sign on if Kimberlee was replaced by a different actress. Can you believe it?"

"But why?" asked Odelia. "Why would she do such a thing?"

"Isn't it obvious? Jealousy, pure and simple. Kim is an up-and-coming talent, who's about to make it big, and Emerald a has-been on her way down."

"So what happened?"

"So Alina and Abbey flatly refused to fire Kim. Said she was an integral part of the cast and if Kim walked, they would walk, too. And since they're co-producing, Emerald didn't have a leg to stand on."

"She could have bowed out."

"No, she couldn't. She's not getting the parts she used to,

and she needs the work. The show was last year's biggest hit, and was shaping up to be an even bigger hit this year, so Emerald wanted in, whatever the cost."

"Even if she had to tolerate Kimberlee," said Odelia, nodding.

"Exactamundo."

"What happened just now with Verna Rectrix?" asked Chase.

"Actors," he said with a shrug. "They're all nuts."

He quickly excused himself and moved off.

"If you ask me, there's more to this Verna story than Kimberlee's boyfriend is letting on," said Chase.

"Definitely. Who would have thought there was so much dirt to dig up?"

"And all off the record," said Chase with a grin.

"Absolutely. I have a hunch this whole weekend is going to be one long feast of off-the-record stories."

Chase studied her for a moment. "You're having fun, aren't you?"

"Detective Kingsley," she said dramatically, placing a hand on his arm and gesturing around at the little cliques of gossiping Hollywood actors and their significant others, "this is what paradise looks like to a reporter."

# CHAPTER 8

*I*n the daytime Kingman can always be found on Main Street, where he holds court in front of his human's popular store. Now, in the middle of the night, for some reason the general store is closed for business, and so Kingman shifts his presence to the park, where most of Hampton Cove's cats meet up.

We like to call it cat choir, because we have a regular conductor, who tries to tell us what to do, and tries to instill a modicum of melodiousness in the ragtag collection of cats' wailings. But as Shanille well knows, it's all to no avail. Cats can't sing, and that's the hard truth of the matter. We do know how to produce a lot of noise, and we enjoy it, too, especially in the springtime, when males and females try to attract each other's attention for procreational purposes, which is what Harriet's beef with Brutus apparently was all about.

So after a short hike we arrived at the park, and immediately I felt buoyed, just like Dooley had promised. My friend was right. When a cat wants to forget about his trouble with humans, all he or she needs to do is spend some time amongst his own posse, and those lingering doubts and fears all melt like snow before the summer sun. It didn't hurt that Brutus's troubles were greater than my own, which offered a welcome distraction. The soap opera principle.

"Kingman—hey, Kingman!" I called out when I caught sight of our trusty old comrade.

As usual, he was perched on top of the jungle gym, which offers a bird's-eye view of the goings-on in the park. Or should I say a cat's-eye view?

Cat choir convenes at the children's playground. It consists of a swing, a jungle gym, and other paraphernalia designed to entertain and delight infant humans, all bolted to the ground and finished with a nice layer of rubber.

During the daytime it is overrun with children, watched over by their doting parents, but once darkness sets in, cats take over and rule this roost.

We'd joined Kingman, who was chatting up two very perky-looking cats, and he reluctantly transferred his attention to us. A spreading piebald, he is by way of being Hampton Cove's feline mayor, and one of my oldest friends.

"You won't believe this," he said, "but now Shanille has gotten it into her nut that cat choir needs fresh blood, so she's asked her cousin Minny, who lives over in Happy Bays, to send some of that town's cats over here." He shook his head. "As if we don't have enough trouble laying down the law with this sorry lot." He gestured vaguely in the direction of the three dozen or so cats who were shooting the breeze, preparatory to starting rehearsals.

"Yeah, that's all very interesting," I said, not interested in the finer points of cat choir organization right then. "The thing is, we need your help, Kingman."

"Okay. What is it this time? Has Dooley seen UFOs? Is he worried again about the end of the world?"

"UFOs?" asked Dooley. "What are UFOs?"

"Nothing," I said, not wanting to get sidetracked. "Brutus needs a shrink, Kingman, and we were hoping you could recommend him one."

Kingman stared at me for a moment, then roared with laughter, his voluminous belly quivering like jelly. "Max!" he cried, tears rolling down his furry cheeks. "That's the most hilarious thing I've ever heard! A shrink! For cats!"

I wasn't laughing, though, and neither were Harriet and Brutus. Dooley, of course, laughed right along, even though he probably had no idea what he was laughing about. He's every sociable that way.

Finally it dawned on Kingman that we were deadly serious. "You're not kidding," he said, wiping the tears from his eyes. He turned his attention to a somber-looking Brutus and Harriet. "Lovers' tiff? Is that's what's going on here?"

"Not exactly," I said. "Brutus. You better tell him."

"I'm having doubts," said Brutus.

"Doubts? Doubts about what?"

"I'm not so sure if deep down I'm not a female rather than a male," said Brutus, darting a quick glance around to make sure no one overheard him. This was deep stuff, and he didn't need cat choir members making fun of him.

Kingman blinked. "Wait, let me get this straight. You think that deep down you might be a female and not a male?"

"That's right."

"Who gave you that idea?!" Kingman cried, and looked as if he were on the verge of another bout of hilarity.

"No one," said Brutus gruffly. "I discovered this all by myself."

"Well, you did see that Discovery Channel documentary," I reminded him.

"Yeah, but that only served to remind me of a truth I always knew I knew. On a subconscious level, if you see what I mean. In my heart of hearts."

"Oh, my God," said Harriet, rolling her eyes.

"It did!" said Brutus.

"Brutus is confused," I said, "so we thought he should probably talk to a shrink." I was walking on eggshells, Brutus's foul glances and grumpy face warning me he might explode at any moment, like one of those volcanoes that suddenly erupt and slay a town full of unsuspecting natives.

"Look, I don't know no shrink," said Kingman. "In fact I don't think I've ever heard of a cat needing a shrink before, but what I can tell you is that you need to talk this thing through with your girlfriend. I mean, how do *you* feel about all of this, Harriet?"

"I think it's ridiculous. Brutus is the manliest cat I've ever met. And now for him to suddenly think he's a female deep inside is just ridiculous." She gave Brutus a slap. "Just get over yourself, Brutus. Get your head straight."

"My head is straight," said Brutus gruffly. "And for your information, I can't help what I feel, can I? And if I feel like deep inside there's a female waiting to burst out, then there's a frickin' female waiting to burst out."

"Sounds more like one of them *Alien* movies to me," said Kingman.

But Harriet wasn't finished. "And listen to this, Kingman. Now he's trying to convince me that deep down inside I'm actually a male and he's a female and we need to do some kind of switcheroo thing. Isn't that the most ridiculous thing you've ever heard? Me! A male!"

"Yeah, well," Kingman said, rubbing his chin. "Then again, we have to respect Brutus's feelings on this, Harriet, so if he really feels he's a female…"

"Exactly!" said Brutus, vindicated now that a person with authority like Kingman decided to back him up. "You can't argue with feelings, snookie."

"Don't call me snookie. And how about babies, huh? How

about starting a family? How am I supposed to have babies now, with you wanting to have your equipment... rearranged? Max, tell Kingman what you told us."

"About the..."

"Operation."

Brutus gulped at the mention of the word. He might have a female waiting to burst out of him, but he clearly wasn't ready to give her the all-clear.

"If Brutus is serious about turning into a female, he should probably have an operation," I told Kingman. "Humans do it all the time. Women turn into men and men into women and sometimes, just for the fun of it, they change their minds and do it all over again. It's a very common thing these days."

"But if he does that, how are we ever going to have babies!" Harriet cried. "It's just not fair!"

Kingman cleared his throat. "Babies?" he said. "You want babies?"

"Well, maybe not right now, but at some point, sure. Who doesn't?"

Kingman coughed. "Um, and how do you feel about this, Brutus?"

"Well, of course I want to have babies, too, but maybe first we should do the switcheroo thing. So I'll have the babies and Harriet will do... the other bit." He didn't seem entirely sure about this part, though, for I had the impression he'd gone a little white around the nostrils. Tough to tell, though, with all of that black fur.

Kingman coughed again.

"Are you coming down with something, Kingman?" asked Dooley.

"No, no, I'm fine," said Kingman. "It just strikes me as odd that Odelia never gave you... the talk."

"The talk?" I said. "What talk?"

"Well, *the* talk. About…" He made a gesture as if cutting a piece of twine with his claws. "Snip-snip."

"Snip-snip?" I said, not comprehending.

He groaned. "Oh, boy. Y'all better sit down for this one." We all sat down. Then Kingman took a deep breath. "Max and Dooley—you were both neutered as infants. And you, Harriet, were spayed. I'm not sure about you, Brutus, as you're new in town, but every kitten born in Hampton Cove is neutered or spayed as a rule. No exceptions. They're pretty strict about it."

We stared at him, not comprehending. I smiled, confused. "What are you talking about? What is this 'neutering' thing? Or the 'spaying?'"

"Odelia should have told you—you've all been fixed."

I still didn't get it. "Fixed? Fixed for what?"

"You can't have babies, all right? Trust me on this—you just can't!"

As the horrible truth dawned upon us, our collective jaws dropped.

"WHAT?!!!!!" we all yelled simultaneously.

# CHAPTER 9

*T*he evening wound down shortly after midnight, when Emerald decided to call it a night. And even though she insisted her guests stay and have a good time, her departure was the cue for the others to retire to bed soon after.

Odelia was actually glad to hit the hay. She'd probably had a few glasses too much to drink, and the prospect of her head hitting the hay, not to mention that appealingly soft, downy pillow, was suddenly very appealing.

"Well, that was quite an evening," said Chase as he took off his shirt.

The room was an opulent one, with a hardwood floor, a four-poster bed, and pink silk wallpaper. The bathroom, which was the first thing Odelia had checked upon arrival, actually had golden taps and a white marble bathtub.

"So what's on the program for tomorrow? asked Chase.

Next to the bed, on the nightstand, lay the weekend's itinerary. "Friday night welcome dinner, Saturday morning breakfast then a game of croquet," she read. "Huh. Croquet.

Is that what the rich get up to when they have some time to kill?"

"Sounds good to me," said Chase. "I could use the action." He patted his belly, which was a little bloated after the feast they'd just enjoyed.

Odelia had a hard time dragging her eyes away from Chase's torso and back to the itinerary. "Saturday night is movie time at the Cinema Emerald."

"Of course Emerald would have a home theater," said Chase, throwing himself onto the bed, his hands behind his head.

"I wonder what movie she'll show."

"Probably something from her own long and illustrious career."

"Probably," Odelia agreed. She remembered what Kimberlee's boyfriend had told them about Emerald not being sincere when she spoke about announcing Kimberlee as the successor to her acting crown.

"And now," she said, yawning and stretching, "I think I could do with some sleep."

Chase took her by the waist and dragged her down on the bed. "But first... dessert," he grunted, and kissed her.

She giggled. "Wouldn't that be something? Making love under Emerald Rhone's roof. Something to tell the grandkids one day."

"I'd love to tell the grandkids," Chase murmured.

She gazed lovingly up into his handsome face and placed a hand on his cheek. She was tired, but not that tired, and then they kissed again, slower and with more passion this time.

And they would have kept on kissing—and maybe something more—if there hadn't been a loud ruckus just outside their door. It kinda ruined the moment.

"I know what you're up to, you horrible dirtbag!"

someone was screaming. It was a woman's voice, and it sounded a lot like... Alina Isman.

Odelia opened the door a crack and peered out. Right outside their door, Alina and her husband Reinhart were arguing loudly, Alina dressed in a sheer negligee, and her husband in striped boxers and nothing else.

"I was only going down for a nightcap, I swear!" the singer cried.

"Nightcap, my ass! You were going to fool around with that floozie!" the redheaded actress screamed. She slapped his chest. "Admit it, you bastard!"

"Uh-oh," said Chase. "Busted."

"I wonder what floozie she's talking about," whispered Odelia.

More doors opened up and down the hall, and Alina and her husband now had an audience. She didn't seem to care, for she kept laying into Reinhart. The latter tried to neutralize the situation by holding up his hands and producing a nothing-to-see-here-folks smile, but it was obvious he'd been busted.

Suddenly another voice joined the chorus. "What's going on here?"

It was Emerald, and she looked ready to go to bed, her hair mussed up, her nightgown casually wrapped around herself, her face make-up free now. She was beautiful, Odelia thought. Even at seventy she had that amazing bone structure that's the hallmark of true ageless beauty.

"He was sneaking downstairs to meet that, that... slut!" Alina cried, her voice shrill.

"I was only going for a nightcap!" said Reinhart. "I swear on our children, Alina! I swear!"

"Don't you dare!" she cried, wagging a finger in her husband's face. She was shaking, her eyes shooting fire, her face a mask of fury.

Odelia wondered if this was all a performance or if it was for real. At any rate, Alina was an amazing actress. Odelia didn't think she could ever get this emotional with a dozen people standing around. She'd probably feel too self-conscious and pipe down the moment she knew she had an audience. But not Alina. It was almost as if having an audience fueled the flame of her anger.

Suddenly, Alina's fury turned from her husband to a young woman who'd just joined them. Kimberlee was dressed in colorful PJs and looked absolutely adorable, Odelia thought.

"Don't think I don't know what you've been up to behind my back," Alina snarled.

"I honestly have no idea what you're talking about," said Kimberlee, her face impassive.

"You seduced my husband! My husband—my rock—you took him from me!" Alina was clutching a fist to her heart, pounding her chest.

"Oh, she's good," said Chase. "She's very good."

"I didn't take your husband, Alina," said Kimberlee. "I swear to God. I would never—"

"Liar!" Alina bellowed. "Cheat!" she added when her husband tried to place his hands on her shoulders and she slapped them away. "Oh, I know how it is. Dump the old girl and replace her with a younger model—but you're not replacing me, buster! I'm leaving you! And I'm taking the kids!"

"But honey!"

"You brought this all on yourself—I'm divorcing you, Reinhart. Do you hear me? I've had enough of your philandering and your lying and your cheating. And you," she added, viciously turning on Kimberlee. "You stole my husband—you try to steal my career—laughing behind my back—making cracks about my age and decaying beauty! 'Oh, she's lost it. She's a wreck.'"

"But Alina, I never—"

"Shut up!" Alina screeched. "Shut up shut up shut up!"

"If this were a movie, someone would slap her," said Chase.

"Only if this were a movie from the forties," said Odelia.

But it wasn't a movie, from the forties or otherwise, so no one slapped anyone, and a good thing, too, cause it would only make matters worse.

"I'm going to bed," said Alina suddenly. "And you can sleep in *her* bed for all I care!" she added, pointing an accusing finger at Kimberlee.

Kimberlee was shaking her head, looking distraught. Alina's husband, meanwhile, hurried after his wife. "But, Alina!"

"I've had it with you! You can find your own way home!"

And then she slammed the door in his face and he stood there for a moment, staring at the door, as if he couldn't quite believe what had just happened. He then pounded the door with his fist. "Alina! Alina, sweet pea!"

Emerald stepped forward and placed a hand on his shoulder. "Reinhart, I'll find you another room. You can sort this all out in the morning."

He nodded and followed her, looking like a beaten man.

Gradually, the others all filed back into their respective rooms, and so did Odelia and Chase.

"What a circus," said Chase.

"I really had no idea they were as passionate in their personal lives as they are on the screen," said Odelia as they got into bed.

"Passionate? Berserk, you mean."

She snuggled up to Chase. Neither of them was in the

mood for nookie now, so she just lay there, going over the events of the evening in her mind.

And she'd just nodded off when her phone chimed. Dazedly, she picked it from the nightstand. The first thing she heard was the voice of her grandmother.

"Odelia, honey, I'm sorry to wake you, but the little ones are going nuts."

And then she heard the voice of Max, clear as a bell in her ear.

"You had us NEUTERED???!!!!!"

# CHAPTER 10

"Wait, I thought you knew."

"No, we most certainly did not know!" I said.

It had come as something of a shock when Kingman broke the news to us that we were... that way. The snip, he called it, and the word made me shiver. Snipped! Someone—probably Vena, who I could totally see doing a horrible thing like that—snipped something where nothing should have been snipped!

"And what about me?" said Harriet, struggling to get to the phone. "It was that Vena woman, wasn't it? She did this to me! She turned me into a travesty of what a cat should be!"

"But you guys!" Odelia cried. She sounded weird. As if she'd just woke up. Which probably made sense. Humans like to sleep at night. A weird habit, if you ask me, and probably unhealthy. Nighttime is prowling time, after all.

"This snipping thing," said Dooley. "Did it hurt? Cause I can't remember."

"It happened when you were very young," said Odelia.

"And no, it didn't hurt. Vets always use anesthesia when they perform the procedure."

"I'm pretty sure I wasn't snipped," said Brutus gruffly. "Kingman said as much. He said he couldn't be sure, and I'd remember if someone tried to mess with my plumbing. In fact I'd give them a punch in the snoot if they so much as tried to touch me down there, vet or no vet. I don't stand for nonsense."

"Look, this is better for you," said Odelia. "For one thing it prevents you from spraying urine all over the house. It also—"

"Spraying!" I cried. "I would never lower myself to such a foul practice!"

"Well, that's because of the snip," said Odelia.

"But Odelia! You could have at least asked!"

"Who are you talking to?" a voice sounded on the other end. I recognized it as Chase, who was probably wondering what all this talk of snipping and spraying meant—in the middle of the night.

"My grandmother. She, um, had something urgent that couldn't wait."

"If she's spraying urine all over the house she should probably talk to your dad."

"It's not—I wasn't…"

"Hey, it's nothing for your grandmother to be embarrassed about, babe. When you get to a certain age, these things happen."

"Chase…"

"One word. Adult diapers. Actually, that's two words."

Gran, who'd been slowly turning red in the face now cried, "Hey, for your information I'm housebroken, young man!"

"Actually she wasn't asking for herself," said Odelia. "She's talking about my cats."

"Your cats!"

"Yeah, she couldn't remember if they were neutered or not."

"Neutered." I shivered violently. "Neutered!"

"It's just a word, honey," said Gran, gently stroking my fur.

"It sounds horrible—like something from a horror movie!"

"More like from an action movie," said Brutus, who loved his action movies of an evening. He assumed a fighting position, paws up. "I'll neuter you." He grinned. "Sounds like a catchphrase Bruce would use." He threw a few air punches. "If you don't stop acting like a total tool, I'll neuter you."

"If *you* don't stop acting like a fool, I'll neuter *you*," I said, and I meant it.

"Look, it's not as if you were ever going to have babies, were you, Max?" said Brutus, who was more relaxed now that he knew he hadn't been 'fixed.'

"What makes you say that?" I said.

"Well…" He hesitated. "I mean, how long have we known each other? Couple of months? And in all that time never once have I seen you with a girl."

"So?"

"So I just assumed…"

"You assumed what?" I said. I didn't have time for this. I needed to get to the bottom of this snipping business.

"Well, I just assumed you weren't into them is all."

I stared at him. "What?!"

He shrugged. "Call it a hunch. And seeing as how you and Dooley are so close and all I naturally assumed…" His voice died away as I gave him my best imitation of a death stare. "No? Okay, then."

"For your information, I simply haven't found the right

one yet. And also for your information, Dooley and I are just friends, nothing more."

"What is he talking about, Max?" asked Dooley. "What is he implying?"

"He's implying that you and I are more than just friends," I said.

Dooley thought about this for a moment. "What more is there?"

"Oh, will you just go away, Dooley," said Harriet. She moved closer to the phone. "So this thing is reversible, right? It is, isn't it? Reversible?"

"I guess... I'm not sure," said Odelia, sounding reluctant to explore this avenue.

"I knew it! So we'll just have it reversed, and Brutus can get over his little issue and then we'll have a nice big litter, just like I've always wanted."

"What little issue?" asked Odelia.

"Oh, nothing serious," said Harriet. "He just thinks that deep down he's a female, not a male."

"Wait, what?"

"Can we please discuss all this when you get back?" said Gran, yawning.

"Just a minute—can my thing be reversed, too?" I asked.

"Um..." said Odelia.

A male voice intruded upon her eloquence. "Gran? Hi, Chase here. Look, I'm sorry about the misunderstanding. Got our wires crossed for a minute there."

"No need to apologize, Chase," said Gran. "I can see how all this must be very confusing to you."

"The thing is, all this talk about snipping and neutering and spaying? I mean, can't this wait until tomorrow? We have croquet in the morning."

"What did he say?" I asked.

"They're having croque-monsieur in the morning," said Gran.

"Not croque-monsieur. Croquet. It's a sport."

"Oh, I get it," said Gran, giving me a wink for some reason. "Is that what you young people call it these days? Good to know. I like some croquet myself from time to time. Which reminds me, I should call Dick. He asked me out on a date last week and I haven't gotten back to him. Do you know Dick Bernstein? From the senior center? He's sweet on me. Him and Rock Horowitz both."

"Look, why don't we discuss all this when I get back," said Odelia, taking over the phone again.

"Sure thing, honey," said Gran. "Rock and Dick can wait."

"So about this snippy thing," said Dooley, jostling to get closer to the phone, "it can be reversed, right? In that case I'll have a reversal, too."

"We'll all have reversals," I said. "Reversals for everyone, please, Odelia."

"Except for me," said Brutus, flicking an imaginary speck of dust from his chest. "No reversals needed for The Brutus."

"Gran," Chase said. "Hi. Chase again. Why are we still talking?"

With one eye on Brutus, Gran said, "Quick question. Do you remember if Brutus was neutered as a kitten?"

"Of course he was," Chase said. "First thing my mom did when she got him. Neutered, dewormed, vaccinated and chipped. And now can we finally get back to sleep?"

Brutus's jaw dropped. "Wait, what?"

"Don't worry—the whole thing is totally reversible," I said.

"You neutered me?!" Brutus yelled into the phone. "Are you crazy?"

"I didn't neuter you, Brutus," said Odelia. "That was Chase's mom."

"Wait, are you talking to Brutus now?" asked Chase. "God, I must be dreaming. This is all a dream, right? Am I dreaming?"

"You tell Chase to tell his mom there's such a thing as my body—my choice!" Brutus yelled. "Tell him!"

"It'll all work out fine," said Odelia.

"My body—my choice!" Brutus cried.

"Hey, maybe this is a good thing," said Dooley. "You wanted to be turned from a male into a female, right? Well, you're halfway there, Brutus. They neutered you, so now it's only one small step to becoming a real female!"

Brutus looked like he was about to murder Dooley, and I had the distinct impression his doubts about his inner male or female had suddenly taken a backseat—and no shrinks had been harmed in the process!

"I think it's a rotten thing to do, Odelia," Brutus growled into the phone. "And I'm disappointed, you hear me? Disappointed!"

"But, Brutus," said Dooley. "This is a good thing!"

"Yes, Brutus," Odelia said. "Look on the bright—"

"Very disappointed!" he screamed, and hit the Disconnect button.

"Finally," Gran muttered, and promptly dozed off, phone still in her hand.

"My body—my choice," Brutus repeated, as if it were his new mantra.

"So we're all in the same boat," said Harriet. "All of us have been badly betrayed by our masters." Her face took on a mutinous expression. "I suggest we teach them a lesson. I suggest we elope. Right now!"

"Elope!" said Dooley. "But..."

"They had a duty of care, Dooley—and they blew it! They removed a vital part of our anatomy without our permission. There are laws against that kind of thing. In fact

I'm pretty sure Odelia and the others can be arrested for this."

"Arrested?" asked Dooley, taken aback.

She ticked the items off on her claws. "Cat mutilation. Violation of our immutable rights under the Universal Declaration of Feline Rights. Gross negligence... Do I really have to go on?"

"I doubt whether Uncle Alec will arrest his niece, his sister and his mother for cat mutilation," I said.

"So we elope!" said Harriet. "We teach them a lesson they won't forget!"

"And what lesson would that be?"

"That they should think twice before sending us to Vena the Butcher!"

"I doubt Odelia will get the message," I said. "She's so busy playing croque-monsieur with Chase that she won't even know we're gone."

"But the others will. Marge, Gran..."

We looked at Gran, who was sleeping with her mouth open, snoring softly.

"I don't think Gran is going to miss us terribly," said Dooley softly.

"Oh, for Pete's sake," I said. "I agree they should never have done this to us, but if we elope now we'll only be punishing ourselves. Just think—no soft couch to sleep on, no food, fresh water, litter box..."

Harriet thought for a moment, then that mutinous look was back. "Fine. If you won't do it, I will. As of this moment, I'm eloping, and if you have even an inch of self-respect left in your snipped bodies, you'll follow my lead."

And then she set off. Brutus, Dooley and I shared a look. "I'm going with her," said Brutus. "I mean, that's my woman. I have to stand by her. For better, for worse, for richer, for poorer, in sickness and in health, until—"

"Oh, for crying out loud, Brutus," I said. "You're not married, man."

"See you, guys," he said. And off he went, standing by his woman.

We stared after them, and soon we heard the pet flap flap.

I turned to Dooley. "So how about it, buddy? Are we eloping or not?"

He darted a glance at his favorite spot at the foot of Gran's bed. It was nice and soft and extremely inviting. Finally he said, "Ok, fine. Let's elope. But not for too long, all right? I kinda like our humans—even if they did remove a part of our anatomy that they probably shouldn't have without our permission."

"Your objections are duly noted," I said, and then we eloped—reluctantly.

# CHAPTER 11

*T*he next morning, bright and early, Odelia awoke to music streaming from hidden speakers. At first she thought she was in her own bed at home, and her first instinct was to feel for the trusty shape of Max sleeping at her feet. Max would usually, and sometimes even before she was fully awake, crawl up to her armpit, bury his nose under her arm, and purr up a storm. He'd been doing this ever since he was a kitten and still performed this early morning ritual without fault. Sometimes he exchanged her armpit for her elbow or her neck but he always had to have this morning cuddle. He would knead the blanket, or sometimes Chase's arm if it was closer, not bothering to retract his claws, which would sometimes elicit a few choice curse words from Chase.

And then, when he had enough, he would suddenly get up and scoot off as fast as he could. It was a weird but adorable little ritual and she missed it now.

Next to her, Chase stirred, so she put his head under her armpit. He got the idea, and was soon purring himself. They both laughed, and listened to the music for a moment.

"Is that... Barbra Streisand?" asked Chase, his voice muffled.

*'Memory, all alone in the moonlight,'* Barbra wailed from the speakers.

"I think it is," said Odelia, stretching luxuriously, then throwing back the comforter and swinging her feet to the floor. She bunched up her toes and kneaded the high-pile carpet for a moment. "Nice," she murmured.

"You don't say," said Chase, who was doing the same thing on his side of the bed. "So what was all that about your grandmother wanting to know if Brutus was neutered?" he asked. "Did that really happen or was I dreaming?"

"Oh, you know Gran. She's a little eccentric sometimes."

"More like completely stark-raving mad," he grunted.

Odelia frankly was a little worried. It had never occurred to her to let her cats know they'd been spayed or neutered or whatever it was called. And now they knew—she wondered how. Probably some other cats had told them.

"Good morning all you lovelies!" Emerald's voice suddenly boomed through the room. "Welcome to your first full day of fun and friendship at Casa Emerald! A delicious breakfast buffet is served in the morning room so I'll see you all there. Oh, and I have a little surprise for you. No, I'm not telling you what it is. You'll have to come down and see for yourself. So rise and shine, you adorable sleepyheads, and I'll see you in a few ticks!"

"She's like the happy, peppy hostess from hell," Chase groaned as he rubbed his face.

After the commotion with Alina freaking out about her husband having an affair with Kimberlee last night, and then the phone call about her cats freaking out about having been neutered in the middle of the night, Odelia and Chase hadn't exactly enjoyed a good night's sleep. Still Odelia felt energized. She had a hard time believing she was sleeping under

Emerald Rhone's roof, sharing a weekend with the screen goddess and her friends!

They quickly showered, got dressed, and proceeded downstairs in search of the promised breakfast buffet and, of course, Emerald's 'little surprise.'

"I'll bet it's jewelry," said Odelia as they walked down the stairs. "An expensive watch for the men and earrings for the women. Or maybe bracelets for the women and cufflinks or blazer buttons for the men! Or both!"

"Whatever it is, I hope Emerald makes a strong coffee," grunted Chase. "I feel like I'm still half asleep and won't be fully awake until I've had my first hit of caffeine."

Just like the night before, they were greeted at the bottom of the stairs by the same liveried servant. This time he ushered them into the morning room. Located near the back of the house, its French windows, which were all open, offered a stunning view of the pool area and the smooth lawns behind it.

"Imagine having your own private swimming pool," said Odelia as she walked over to the window and marveled at that delicious expanse of cooling blue. "I would definitely go for a swim every morning, without fail."

"Yeah, me, too," said Chase, placing an arm across her shoulders. "I guess our teeny tiny backyard is too small for a pool, though, right?"

"We could put in a birdbath."

He laughed. "It's not exactly the same thing."

"Almost but not exactly," she agreed.

Several of the guests sauntered in, with others already tucking into their breakfast. Alina was eating by herself, Reinhart on the other side of the room, and Verna looked much the worse for wear, with bags under her eyes, as she munched on a bagel and sipped from a smoothie, Thaw Roman by her side. Kimberlee and Zoltan walked in, engaged in conversation, and Abbey and Seger were checking out the breakfast buffet. The only ones missing were Emerald and Pete. Then again, a diva always arrives fashionably late and likes to make a grand entrance. Maybe she was preparing her surprise!

Odelia joined Abbey at the buffet.

"Oh, hey," said Abbey jovially. "Sleep well?"

"As well as can be expected," said Odelia truthfully.

"Yeah, what a show last night, huh?" She darted a quick glance at Alina, who was looking like the original ice queen, her back ramrod straight and her green eyes shooting sheets of flame in the direction of her errant husband.

"Do you really think Reinhart was sneaking off for some midnight nookie with Kimberlee?" asked Odelia, keeping her voice down.

Abbey snorted. "Midnight nookie. I like that. It's possible. Kimberlee did have a reputation on set for being a little... morally flawed, shall we say."

"You mean she had an affair with a member of the crew?"

"Several members, allegedly. The only one I'm sure about is our fearless director."

"She had an affair with the director?"

"I know, right. Talk about a cliché."

"So what did her boyfriend say?"

"I don't think he knows. You know what they say: what happens on set, stays on set."

Odelia wondered if she should point out that Abbey was breaking this very rule right now but thought better of it.

"We used to be besties, you know," said Abbey, as she transferred a bagel and a slice of Brie on to her plate. "The original BFFs."

"You and Kimberlee?"

Abbey nodded. "Thick as thieves all through the filming of the first season."

"So what happened?"

"She dumped me."

"Dumped you—as in…"

"As in one day out of the blue she decided she liked Verna better than me, so from one day to the next she started ghosting me and hanging out with Verna. No idea why. I guess she figured Verna was more fun to be around than little old me. They are the same age, of course, while I'm just an old hag."

"You're not an old hag," said Odelia, then remembered that Abbey was in her forties now. It's hard to imagine that the heroes of your youth age, too. She'd seen Abbey Moret play the peppy ditzy blonde in so many movies it was hard to imagine she was a forty-year-old mom now, not a teenager.

"But you know, who cares?" said Abbey, though it was obvious she cared a great deal. "It's not as if I'll be seeing the jezebel for much longer. After this weekend is over, it's sayonara, stupid cow, and good riddance." And with these words, she returned to her table with her tray.

"What was that all about?" asked Chase.

"Apparently Alina isn't the only one who hates Kimberlee. Abbey does, too."

"My God," said Chase. "It's like high school all over again, isn't it?"

"Just human nature, I guess."

"Human nature, my foot. I work with the same people year-round and I never get into screaming matches or blow my top. You know what I think?"

"I'm sure you're about to tell me."

"Big egos clashing. Put one movie star in a movie with a bunch of nobodies, and everyone gets along great. Put five movie stars together and fireworks are guaranteed."

"I don't know about that. Sometimes the most successful people have the smallest egos."

"You don't believe that."

"I do, actually. Just look at Emerald. She's so gracious and so humble. Not the diva I thought she would be at all."

Chase eyed her curiously. "Are you seriously calling Emerald Rhone a humble person?"

"Down-to-earth, unassuming, kind—in a word, humble."

They'd taken a seat and devoted themselves to the items on their plates. "I disagree," he said. "She's the classic diva, and all these other divas probably hate her guts and she loves it."

Like last night, the food once again was to die for: there were so many different choices on display that Odelia was sorry she only had one stomach. She took a sip from her freshly squeezed orange juice and took a bite from her buttermilk pancakes with maple syrup and some of that sautéed spinach.

Chase, meanwhile, attacked his hash brown potatoes, blueberry pancakes, streaky crisp pork bacon and roast honey glazed ham with French toast while sipping from his piping hot and spoon-standing-up strong black coffee.

"I think Emerald has managed to stay with both feet firmly planted in reality—a regular person like the rest of us mere mortals, and I've always admired that about her," said Odelia.

Just then, the doors to the breakfast room swung open and Emerald burst in. She was looking resplendent in an Adidas tracksuit, and had a brilliant smile plastered across her face. "Hello, my beloved friends!" she cried. "I trust you've all had a wonderful night. And I trust all differences have been put firmly aside." She cast a meaningful look at Alina and Reinhart, neither of whom reacted. "I'm not going to keep you in suspense. It's time for your gift!"

"Whoopsie," said Odelia, putting her hands together and joining in the applause.

Chase was already removing his watch to make a place for the new and snazzier one he was sure to receive.

Emerald clapped her hands and a cart was rolled in by two servers, overseen by Emerald's husband Pete. On the cart cans of Coke had been piled in a nice pyramid.

"Ta-dah!" Emerald sang on a high note, an excited trill in her voice.

Everyone stared at the cans of Coke.

Chase started putting his watch back on.

Emerald picked up the top can and showed it to her stunned guests. "Coke Emerald! The Coca-Cola Company has created a new Coke especially for me! It tastes a little sweeter than classic Coke, with a minty aftertaste, not unlike myself," she said with a wink at her husband, who looked appropriately embarrassed. "Go on, try it," she said, and started handing out the cans. "There's plenty for everyone, so take as many as you want. They won't be in stores until the fall so this is a real treat for you and your loved ones."

Chase took a can from the servers who'd started distributing the cans among the guests, who all accepted the unique gift with the requisite murmurs of appreciation, while still looking slightly stunned and baffled.

Chase turned the can over in his hand, then opened it with a pop and took a swig. "Tastes like Coke," he said. "Like she said—a little sweeter."

Underneath the Coke logo the name Emerald had been added, and a green-and-gold stripe added to the famous swoosh. Odelia caught Chase's eye and they both had to suppress a snort of laughter. So no watches, bracelets or earrings but cans of Coke. Ah, well, she thought. At least she had something to write home about. Literally.

CHAPTER 12

"Do you think they're missing us already?" asked Dooley.

We'd spent the night in the park, not far from cat choir's rehearsal spot. Of course all of cat choir's members had gone home by now, to their respective couches and beds and extra-soft and fluffy pillows, and to their food bowls and litter boxes. The only fools still in the park were the four of us, the elopers.

"I hope so," I said. "I miss my bowl of food."

Gran had developed a habit of putting a little extra snack in our bowls in the morning. Every day was a surprise. One day it could be a slice of sausage or a piece of beef, the next it would be cheese or a cat treat. Gran loved to spoil us. And now that Odelia was gone I knew she'd pull out all the stops and spoil us absolutely rotten. To that purpose she had bought all of the stuff Odelia never got us, because she felt it wasn't healthy or too expensive: all the special gourmet stuff only pampered cats eat. Like us. Except—we'd eloped.

"It's going to take them a while to miss us," said Harriet.

71

"They'll probably just think we went off to the park and will be back when we get tired or hungry."

"I am tired *and* hungry," said Brutus. "And confused," he added for good measure.

"What are you confused about this time?" asked Harriet peevishly. "Don't tell me you think there might be a dog lurking inside of you that hasn't come out yet, or a chicken. Cause I'm going to beat you, Brutus, I swear to God."

"No, I don't think there's a dog or a chicken inside me waiting to burst free," he said, "but I do wonder about my whole purpose as a male if I don't even have a you-know-what to do you-know-what with—if you know what I mean."

Dooley obviously didn't know what he meant, for he said, "What?"

"I don't have a you-know-what and you don't hear me complaining," said Harriet.

"You sure complained a lot about your you-know-what last night," said Brutus.

When Harriet shot him a furious look, he murmured, "Just saying."

"Do you know what a you-know-what is, Max?" asked Dooley.

"Um…"

We were all perched on different branches of the same tree. Not too high up, as we knew from experience it's harder to get down than it is to go up. Cats don't have a reverse gear, you see, and walking down a tree is the same as falling down, which is not advisable. The last time I was high up in a tree the fire department had to come and save me. Not my finest hour.

"And one other thing," said Dooley. "What did Odelia mean when she said that thing about the spraying thing?"

"Male cats spray," said Harriet. "It's one of those dumb things they do. They think it keeps other male cats away—

marks off their territory. Don't ask me why they think it works. Obviously it doesn't."

"And what about female cats? They don't spray?"

"Female cats caterwaul a lot," said Brutus. "They think it attracts male cats. No idea why. Caterwauling isn't an attractive trait if you ask me."

"Nobody asked you," snapped Harriet.

"Dooley did."

"Well, he shouldn't. There are certain things we don't talk about."

"But—"

"Brutus—a lady never tells."

And while Brutus and Harriet bickered, I thought about this spraying business. Odelia didn't have to go and neuter me—or was it spay? If she'd simply told me not to spray, I would have listened. I'm nice like that. But when I said as much to Harriet, who seemed to be an expert on these matters, she said, "It's not something cats have control over, Max. It's instinct."

"Instinct?"

"Yeah, it's built-in behavior. Like rubbing yourself against Odelia's leg."

"I do that to show her how much I care about her."

"You do that because you have scent glands and rubbing spreads your scent, marking off your territory. You're basically telling other cats Odelia is your human so they better stay away or else."

"No, I don't."

"It's instinct, Max—you're not even aware you're doing it."

"I'm absolutely aware. Everything I do, I do for a reason."

"Yeah, right. Like pouncing on a toy mouse."

"It's fun!"

"It's instinct!"

I lapsed into silence. Could there be truth to what she was saying? Was I helpless prey to my own instincts? Hard to believe but there you had it.

"What they shouldn't have done is remove my capacity for procreation," said Harriet now. "If I want to have a litter of kittens, that's my feline right."

"It's not as if there aren't enough cats in the world, though," said Dooley.

"That's not the point and you know it, Dooley," she said. "It's the principle of the thing. Cats have rights, just like any other creature, and humans shouldn't trample all over them just because they can. Like Brutus said, my body—my choice. If I want to have a dozen babies, who's to stop me?"

"Vena Aleman," I muttered. The veterinarian was not our favorite person.

"So as soon as we're home I'm going to ask for that reversal because this is not fair," Harriet continued. It was hard to stop her when she got going.

"I thought we had eloped and were not going home again," I said, confused.

"Pay attention, Max. We're going home once we've taught them a lesson."

"And how long is that going to take?"

She smiled finely. "When they send out search parties and start putting up flyers. That's when we return home with our heads held high and our list of demands. And my number-one demand is to restore my ability to procreate."

"Us males, too?" asked Dooley. "I mean, I don't want to spray everywhere. That's just yucky."

"You're not going to spray now," she said. "You're too old for that crap."

*I* was too old for that crap. I was also too old to spend my days hiding out in trees and hunting for food in back alleys and dumpsters, but I wasn't going to tell her that. Harriet can be very forceful sometimes, and right now I had to admit it was for good reason. Our humans needed to be taught a lesson, and so we were going to teach it, even though it meant making a few sacrifices.

We sat quietly for a moment, watching the sun rise over the park. My stomach was rumbling and my mind drifted to the nice treats Gran would be putting out for us, probably calling our names right now and opening the backdoor to see where we were.

My heart bled for her—and for my poor empty stomach.

CHAPTER 13

*C*roquet was not a sport Odelia had ever played before. In fact she'd had no real awareness of the sport before now. All she knew was that it was played with a wooden hammer and that balls had to be put through hoops hammered into the ground. Clearly none of the other participants in this extravaganza had any idea what they were doing either, which didn't diminish the fun.

Emerald and Pete were both team captains and got to pick their teams—not coincidentally Emerald picked all the women and Pete picked all the men. Soon they were slugging away at those colored balls and putting them through as many hoops as they could. It wasn't exactly a contact sport, but it soon turned into one when Alina faced off against her husband and for a moment Odelia feared she would hit him instead of the ball.

And then she managed to get her revenge by hitting the ball right between Reinhart's eyes. He went down for the count and the game was over before it really got started. A bucket of ice was brought out and Kimberlee's hockey player, who'd seen this type of injury before, attended to the fallen

76

rock star. Alina, impatiently tapping her foot, didn't even pretend to be sorry.

"Nice shot," said Chase as he and Odelia watched the proceedings from the sidelines.

"For a moment there I thought she was going to attack him with the mallet," said Odelia.

"Yeah, that would have been bad."

Kimberlee now also bent down next to Reinhart, like an administering angel holding the ice against the man's damaged snout. When Alina saw this, she took a firmer grip on her mallet and stalked over to Kimberlee. She swung and would have hit the unsuspecting young actress in the back of the head if Pete hadn't been there to stop her at the last moment.

"Let me have a whack at her!" screamed Alina. "Let me have a great big whack at that great big ugly head of hers!" she raged.

"What's your problem, huh?" Kimberlee shouted, now aware she'd narrowly escaped a terrible fate.

"You tart!" Alina screeched. "You horrible little tart!"

"Oh, look who's talking!" Kimberlee screamed right back. "Who tried to seduce my boyfriend, huh? You, you skinny skank!"

"What? Are you crazy?" Alina yelled, balling her fists and shaking them furiously. "I never even came near your stupid boyfriend."

"That's not what he says. He says you came on to him and he had a hard time removing your saggy old boobs from his shoulder!"

For a moment, Alina didn't speak, then suddenly she screamed so loud, Odelia winced, and then she was launching herself at Kimberlee, hands out, claws extended, and tackled the young woman!

For a moment, all Odelia could see were the two ladies

rolling on the floor, screaming so loud even Emerald's distant neighbors must have been alerted by the sound, and then Pete—him again—and Chase and a few of the others managed to separate the two women. There was a rending sound as they were dragged apart, and then Kimberlee stalked off towards the house, minus her shoes, which she had lost in the scuffle, and Alina did the same thing but in the other direction.

"Everyone!" Emerald said nervously. "Drink some more Coke Emerald. There's plenty to go around!" And she held up a can for good measure.

"Who cares about your stupid Coke Emerald, Emerald?!" Abbey yelled. And then she stalked off in the direction of the house, too.

The croquet match was more or less over after that, and people started drifting off in different directions.

"Nice party," said Chase as he joined Odelia.

"It's a miracle these people managed to create two seasons of *Big Little Secrets* without killing each other."

The director of the show, who must have overheard them, drifted over. "Oh, it wasn't like that," he said, "I can assure you."

"They weren't trying to whack each other over the head with croquet mallets?" asked Chase.

The director, a rail-thin man with wavy blond hair and a lined face, smiled indulgently. "No, they weren't. I run a pretty tight ship, and I would have none of this crap. But they wouldn't have gone this far, either. They knew the stakes, and would never spoil the shoot."

"And now that the shoot is over, they just let it all hang out, you mean?" said Odelia.

"Pretty much. A lot of tension is generated when you live cheek by jowl for months on end. It is not a natural state—and it leads to friction."

"So maybe Emerald organized this weekend as a way to get it all out of their system," Odelia suggested.

"I do not think that was her intention per se," said the director, pursing his lips. "It does seem to have a cathartic effect. And who knows? Maybe it is all very, very therapeutic," he added as he picked up a mallet and studied it—possibly for bloodstains.

"At least we have Coke Emerald," said Chase, holding up a can of Coke.

"At least there is that," the director allowed. "By the way, you are not going to print any of this, are you?" he asked, fixing his clear blue eyes on Odelia.

"I have no idea what I'm going to write," she said. "It all depends on my editor and what his expectations are."

"It is going to prove detrimental to these good ladies' reputations if you print the sort of thing that's been going on here. The behind-the-scenes thing."

"Trust me, I'll keep it clean," she said.

He nodded, flashed a quick smile, then rearranged his lined features in a mournful expression, clasped his arms behind his back, and walked off.

# CHAPTER 14

*S*ince the croquet match was canceled due to unforeseen circumstances, Odelia and Chase decided to go for a little stroll through the gardens. The sun was out and Odelia didn't feel like returning to the house to stare at a bunch of mopey faces. So they set foot in the direction Alina had taken and followed her into a mildly wooded area called 'Emerald Forest' according to a sign.

It was where Emerald liked to take her dog for a stroll.

Odelia held her face up to the sun. It was nice to feel the rays touch her skin. They reached the forest and Odelia searched around for Alina. She didn't want to disturb the woman but she did want to make sure she was all right.

"Weird. Do you see her?"

"Nope. She must be deeper in."

So they went deeper in, only to come out the other side two minutes later and come upon a small house that had been built near the perimeter. Still no sign of Alina, though.

"You think she went back to the house?" Odelia asked.

"Either that or she jumped the fence," said Chase, and he wasn't even kidding.

"She's not having the time of her life," Odelia admitted.

"None of these people are, it seems," said Chase. "And they all seem to be harboring a grudge against this Kimberlee Cruz woman."

"This Kimberlee Cruz woman? Don't tell me you don't know who she is?"

"Never heard of her in my life."

"She's quite famous, you know."

"Oh, I'm sure she is, but as long as she isn't in *Die Hard 6* or the new Dwayne Johnson movie, I probably wouldn't know her from Adam."

"Some critics say she could be bigger than Emerald—she's so talented."

"And I'll bet Emerald was delighted to hear that."

"She's a great actress, and she's going to do great things if she keeps this up," said Odelia, who liked Kimberlee, in spite of the stuff Abbey had told her. Then again, she wasn't sure how much of what Abbey had said was true or merely jealous gossip.

"Looks like we've got this place all to ourselves, babe," said Chase as they'd traversed the 'Emerald Forest' from North to South and East to West. They took a seat on a bench that offered a great view of the whole area and relaxed. They sat atop a gently rolling hill, with the main house below them.

"Imagine living in a house like that," said Odelia.

"Not for me, thank you very much."

"Why, too big?"

"For one thing. And too much upkeep. Can you imagine the heating bill?"

Odelia laughed. "Always the practical one, aren't you?"

"It's true! Heating a place like that must cost a pretty penny."

"Not to mention the staff to keep it running."

"At least it's nice to look at."

"And I'm sure Emerald doesn't have trouble footing the bill."

They sat in companionable silence for a while, when suddenly Odelia became aware of screams and shouts that seemed to come from the house. She frowned. "Do you hear that?"

"Yeah, I do. Sounds like Emerald's got yet another crisis on her hands."

"Let's go," she said.

Chase got up with a groan and they walked back to the house at a leisurely pace. "Probably Alina again, trying to kill her husband," he said.

"Or Kimberlee."

They'd arrived at the house when they came upon a distraught-looking Verna Rectrix, who was hugging herself and walking in circles on the terrace. She'd been crying and looked terrible. "What's going on?" asked Odelia.

"A terrible thing," said Verna between sobs. She was rubbing her arms which, Odelia now saw, were covered in tattoos. "I never thought she'd do it and now she did. I still can't believe it—this can't be happening."

"Who did what?" asked Odelia.

"She-she wasn't the type," Verna said, pushing her hands through her dreadlocks. "She wasn't the type but I always said everybody's the type if you push the right buttons. And Alina obviously pushed the right buttons. She did!"

Odelia hugged the woman, and felt Verna's shoulders shake as she burst into a full-blown cry.

"What's going on?" asked Verna's husband Thaw, walking out of the house. "I heard screaming and shouting..." Then he saw his wife and immediately said, "Honey, what's happened?!"

He took over from Odelia and hugged his wife close. "Oh,

she's dead, Thaw! She did it—she finally did it. She killed herself!"

"Who killed herself?" asked Thaw. "Who, Verna—talk to me!"

Verna turned her tear-streaked face up to her husband and sobbed, "Kimberlee. She took a pill and killed herself!"

"What?!" he said, visibly shocked.

Alina's husband now came staggering out of the house. "I don't believe this," he said. "She—she's really dead. It-it's not a joke."

"Kimberlee? Is she…" Thaw asked.

Reinhart nodded distractedly. "She must have done it straight after she returned to the house. Took one of those pills—cyanide. Horrible business—horrible." He took out this phone and walked off, and they could hear him talking into his phone, "Get us the hell out of here, Henry—now!"

Chase and Odelia shared a look, then walked into the house. Taking the stairs two at a time, they arrived at Kimberlee's bedroom. Emerald stood outside the door, her hands balled into fists, pushing her arms against her chest. She'd been crying, her face red, eyes red-rimmed, her nose runny.

"Oh, you can't go in," she said when Chase and Odelia walked up to her. "She—she's dead, you see. Quite dead."

"Yeah, we heard. I'm a cop, Mrs. Rhone," said Chase.

"Oh, you're a cop… Of course you are. Then—by all means—I've called in your colleagues, of course. I've—they'll be here quite soon."

She's totally out of it, Odelia thought, and no wonder.

They entered the room, which looked pretty much like theirs, only twice as big, and immediately saw the body of Kimberlee lying on the floor near the window. Apparently she'd been sitting in a chair, which had fallen down next to her, and had been grasping something. A can of Coke Emerald, which had rolled away, spilling its contents onto the carpet. The poor woman's face was contorted and when Odelia knelt down next to her she got a whiff of almonds.

Chase must have smelled it, too, for he nodded and said, "Cyanide."

Emerald's husband Pete was in the room, and said, "Please don't touch anything. The police will be here soon, and I'm sure they don't want anyone to touch anything..." He swallowed with difficulty, staring at the dead woman.

"It's all right, sir," said Chase. "I'm a cop. Hampton Cove Police Department. And Odelia is one of our civilian consultants. Who found her?"

"Her boyfriend," said Bruce. "Zoltan Falecki. Terrible business. He's completely upset, of course. Imagine finding your loved one like this—terrible business—terrible."

"Where is Zoltan now, Pete?"

"In the salon. We're taking care of him, of course. Making sure he doesn't do something to himself, too. Who would have thought that a young woman, on the brink of global stardom and a stellar career, would ever..."

Odelia took a sniff from the Coke Emerald can, and the same odor filled her nostrils. "The cyanide was in the can," she said. "That's how she must have administered the poison to herself."

"Self-administered cyanide," said Pete. "What a horrible death."

"Yeah, cyanide is not a pleasant way to go," Chase agreed, "but it's quick and effective. The question is—where did she get it? It's not like you can buy this stuff at your local Walgreens."

Discreetly, Odelia took out her phone and snapped a few shots.

"Poor woman," said Pete. "I can't imagine..."

"Where is Alina?" asked Odelia.

"Alina? I don't..."

"It's an obvious question, and one the police will ask, too," said Chase. "Alina was seen almost hitting Kimberlee with a hammer, and now she's dead."

"Surely you're not implying—this is obviously a case of suicide. Very tragic but suicide nonetheless. Alina had nothing whatsoever to do with this..."

"Where is she?" Chase insisted.

"I have absolutely no idea," said Pete, slightly stiffening.

Chase was using his cop voice, and his cop stance, and it differed from the casually laid-back attitude he'd hitherto displayed. He looked a little grim.

"Surely you don't think—I mean Alina is not likely to carry cyanide on her person on the off chance she decides to kill her love rival," said the man with a nervous laugh.

"No, that's not very probable," Odelia admitted.

"I think you better leave now," said Pete, his friendly demeanor quickly waning. "The police will be here soon and they won't like it that we disobeyed a direct order not to let anyone near poor Miss Cruz."

He ushered them out of the room, but not before Odelia took another quick snapshot.

"I hope you're not thinking about publishing those," said Pete, horrified.

"No, of course not," she said, earning herself a slight nod. The door closed, and then they were out.

Behind them, there was a commotion on the stairs, and a large man with a hangdog look on his face came trudging up with some effort. The moment he saw Chase and Odelia his ruddy face broke into a wide smile. "Chase! Odelia! Fancy meeting you here!"

"Uncle Alec!" said Odelia, happy to see her uncle. "I hoped it would be you."

"Of course it's me. Who else are they going to call on a

Saturday morning?" He was still huffing and puffing, catching his breath. "Your mom told me you were off for the weekend—she never told me you'd traded dreary old Hampton Cove for the weekend palaces of the rich and famous?"

"Just a happy coincidence," she said.

"Or an unhappy one," said Chase, indicating the door to Kimberlee's room.

Uncle Alec's face turned grave. "Suicide, huh? Who is she?"

"Kimberlee Cruz."

"Never heard of her," said the Chief. He gestured for Pete to open the door, which Emerald's husband promptly did. Uncle Alec stepped inside, followed by, once again, Chase and Odelia, earning them both a slightly aggravated look from Pete.

"My, my," said Alec as he surveyed the scene, then gave Odelia and Chase a quizzical look. "How long have you two been here?"

"Since last night," said Odelia.

"And already you've got a dead body on your hands."

"We didn't do this, Chief," said Chase.

"I know, I know. But trouble does seem to follow you around." He then crouched down with some effort. "Now let's see what we have here."

$\mathcal{D}$awn had come and we were still sitting in our tree —pretty much in the same spot where we'd settled down the night before.

"Do you think they're looking for us already?" asked Dooley for the umpteenth time.

"I think it's too soon," I answered, also for the umpteenth time.

"Gran does get up early," said Harriet. "She will wonder where we are."

"Maybe we should have waited for a more opportune moment?" I said.

"Like when?"

"Like... when they're all together having dinner? Or watching TV?"

"They'll miss us now for sure," said Harriet. "Gran likes to wake up with Dooley poking his nose in her side, and Marge is the same way with me."

"Nobody wakes up expecting me to snuggle up to them," said Brutus, and he sounded a little annoyed by the fact.

"I'm sure Chase would love you to snuggle up to him," I said.

Brutus scoffed, "Chase would probably kick me out of bed if I tried to pull a stunt like that."

It was true that Chase wasn't exactly cut from the same cloth as Odelia or her mom or gran, but that didn't mean he would exactly kick Brutus out of bed for showing some affection, which is what I told Brutus.

"He has changed," Brutus agreed. "He used to think cats were furry furniture ornaments for old ladies and now he's starting to appreciate us more."

"I wonder if he'll ever be let in on Odelia's little secret, though," I said.

"Not a chance. Outsiders like Chase will never understand the special bond between us cats and the Poole ladies," said Harriet.

"I wouldn't be too sure about that," I said. "Chase has saved our lives several times now—he's part of the family. Isn't that right, Dooley?"

"Chase is Jesus," said Dooley reverently. "Only without the sheep."

"It's true," I said. "Chase is a latter-day Jesus, only without the sheep."

Which was only to be expected. Nobody walks around with a flock of sheep nowadays. It's not very practical.

We were silent for a moment, the only sound interrupting the silence the gentle clicking of our chattering teeth. It gets a little chilly in the park at night, especially after five o'clock in the morning, and we'd all gotten a little shivery.

"And thinking we could be home right now, snuggling up to our humans," said Dooley.

"Be strong, Dooley," said Harriet. "We're teaching them a lesson."

"The very least they could do is pay for the operations,"

said Brutus. "That way I can be a real male again and you can be a real female."

"For your information, I am a real female, even if I'm not a fully functioning one," said Harriet a little snappishly. "But it would be nice if we could have a couple of babies to celebrate our love, sparky star," she added after a pregnant pause.

"My thoughts exactly, sugar biscuit," said Brutus.

"Oh, I'm so sorry I was mean to you, hubby wubby."

"And I'm sorry I went a little cuckoo, bugsie wugsie."

Kissing ensued, and a lot more silly names were bandied about.

"Let's get out of here," I told Dooley after I'd heard all that I could stand.

"Yeah, let's go someplace warm," agreed Dooley, who wasn't a big fan of cuddling couples either.

"I think that's why they do it, you know," I said as we set paw for the nearest bench, so we could sit in the sun and defrost our frozen tushies.

"Do what?"

"Fight? They love to make up so much they will find any excuse to have a fight," I said, gesturing with my head to the couple still holed up in the tree.

"Do you really think so?" said Dooley. "That would explain a lot."

"They do seem to fight for the silliest of reasons nowadays," I said. "Which tells me it's not the fighting they love so much as the making up afterward."

"You could be right," said Dooley. "It seemed weird Brutus would want to turn into a female all of a sudden. He's a very butch cat. Very manly, too."

"He is," I said. "Probably the butchest male I've ever met."

"So you think he made it all up to get into an argument with Harriet?"

"Wouldn't surprise me."

"Couples are weird," said Dooley as we settled in on the park bench.

"And Harriet and Brutus are even weirder."

We watched as the sun cleared the roofs of the houses surrounding the park and warmed our chilly bones. It wasn't the same thing as waking up with my nose dug into Odelia's armpit or neck, pawing her soft and silky hair, but it was better than freezing my tush off in a drafty tree and having to listen to Brutus and Harriet.

"Do you really think they'll come look for us, Max?" Dooley said finally.

"I'm sure of it. They love us, and would never desert us. I mean, isn't that what Odelia keeps telling us?"

"I know she says it, but actions speak louder than words," said Dooley, dispensing a rare nugget of wisdom for once.

So we decided to settle in and wait for our humans to come look for us. I had to say this whole teaching-them-a-lesson thing was proving a lot harder than I'd imagined. It also meant giving up all of our creature comforts, but it was a sacrifice I was willing to make. We could rough it out for a couple of hours—or as long as it took for our humans to become aware of the fact that we'd disappeared.

A school kid was tacking up flyers on trees and lamp-posts, approaching us as he did. Both Dooley and I looked up expectantly.

"This is it, Max," said Dooley excitedly. "They're already putting up flyers telling people to look for us."

The liberally pimpled kid with the carrot hair drew closer and we watched as he tacked a flyer on the lamppost next to our park bench. To my disappointment it didn't depict a nice rendering of my blorange features or Dooley's ragamuffin likeness, or even Harriet's Persian beauty or Brutus's black butchness but an urgent plea to buy one Axe Dark Temptation body spray for men and get a second one for free.

So we sank back down on the bench and decided to wait it out.

It wouldn't be long now.

They'd come looking any minute.

Any minute now...

# CHAPTER 16

*G*ran had been sleeping peacefully when she was awakened by a strange sound. It took her a while to realize the sound was her phone ringing. She frowned, put on her glasses and stared at the ringing annoyance. Finally, she reached out a hand and grabbed the damn thing. If this was a telemarketer trying to interest her in some insurance scheme or one of them damn robocalls, she was going to give them hell—and in case of the robocall she would file another complaint with the FTC—her one hundredth already.

But then she saw it was her granddaughter and her demeanor softened.

"Hey, honey, what are you up to?"

"There's been a death here, Gran. Just wanted to let you know before you saw it on the news. It's got nothing to do with me or Chase—we're both fine."

"A death? What death—who died?"

"One of the actresses committed suicide. She got into a fight with another actress, went to her room and drank a Coke laced with cyanide."

"Strange way to settle an argument," said Gran. "So who is she?"

"Kimberlee Cruz. She was the youngest—about to hit the big time."

"Are you sure it's suicide? Did Emerald Rhone dump the cyanide in her drink so she could wipe out the competition? Hollywood is a tough town."

"Pretty sure. She was alone in her room with the door locked from the inside."

"That doesn't mean a thing," said Gran. "Lemme get dressed. I'll meet you there. It's obvious you're in way over your head and you need my help."

"No, Gran, you don't have to come. In fact please stay home."

"Sounds like you're begging me to come—don't despair. I'm on my way."

"I can handle this. Besides, Chase is here, Uncle Alec is here—it's fine."

"Are you telling your ailing old grandmother that she can't share her final moments with her favorite granddaughter? Is that what you're telling me?"

Odelia groaned, and Gran smiled. Emotional blackmail never failed. When you're an old lady you have to play the cards you're dealt. She then noticed something odd. No cats.

"Have you see Max and Dooley?" she asked.

"Why should I have seen Max and Dooley? They're with you."

"No, they're not. Unless they're downstairs, eating their fill."

They were usually at the foot of the bed, or at least Dooley was, and now that Odelia was gone for the weekend, Max, too, had been extremely affectionate. She'd noticed his affection seemed to follow a hierarchy. Odelia was at the top, and in case she was absent, he shifted his devotion to the number two on his list, which was Gran, then Marge, then Tex, then Chase.

It had been like that since they had him, and the fact that he wasn't there, and nor was Dooley, gave Gran a twinge of worry. Just a twinge, though, for food also featured pretty high on Max's list of priorities. Higher than cuddles.

"They'll probably be downstairs," she repeated. "I'll bring them along. Now that we've got a case to crack we'll need all the help we can get."

"Gran, no!"

But she'd already pressed that big handy red button that meant that whoever was blabbering into her ear could be shut down instantly.

It had taken Gran a while to get used to smartphones but now that she had she never wanted to go back to the day of the rotary dial phone. Besides, she could check the Internet on this phone as well as play video games and call and annoy her friends in one handy device and how cool was that, right?

She swung her feet to the floor, slipped them into her favorite pair of velvety burgundy slippers and stretched. The day was breaking and the sun was already wide awake. So she padded down the stairs, in search of Max and Dooley and the others, so she could give them the good news: they were going on an adventure. One that involved dead Hollywood actresses and cyanide, which was always a fun change from having to take calls from sick people who wanted an appointment with Tex. It was all fine and dandy to be a doctor's receptionist but a girl wants some action from time to time, and this suicide provided just that.

As she arrived downstairs, she saw to her surprise that the four bowls, lined up neatly on the kitchen floor, hadn't been touched. None of them, and the water bowls hadn't been drunk from either.

"What the hell…"

Tex, who came downstairs yawning, white hair standing up on one side of his head and sporting sleep wrinkles on his cheek, muttered, "Morning, Vesta."

"Have you seen the cats?" she asked.

"Cats?" said Tex, as if the concept was a novel one.

"Yeah, the cats. They haven't touched their food and they weren't there when I woke up."

He thought for a moment, trying to wrench his mind to a topic he clearly was reluctant to broach. Finally, he shook his head. "Probably outside. Don't they go to the park at night or something?"

"Yeah, but they should have been back by now. They go to the park at dusk, spend a couple hours there, before hurrying back for a midnight snack and then settling in at the foot of the bed. Max at Odelia's, Dooley alternating between Odelia's and mine, and Brutus and Harriet usually taking up space in your bed." She pointed a bony finger in her son-in-law's direction, practically accusing him of doing away with her cats.

"I didn't see them," he said, holding up his hands in mock surrender. "Have you asked Marge?"

"Oh, don't you worry about Marge—I will ask her. In fact I'll ask her right now. We have a duty of care towards those cats, Tex, and if Odelia finds out they've all gone missing, there will be hell to pay."

Tex didn't seem overly concerned. "They're cats," he said. "Who knows what they're up to?" And he went in search of the coffeemaker, which was right in front of his nose.

Gran went back upstairs and blew into her daughter's room. Marge was still asleep, and when Gran searched around, she found no cats in evidence there, either.

"Where are my cats?!" Gran hollered, and Marge practically flew to the ceiling.

"Who died?!" she cried.

"The cats are gone," said Gran, narrowing her eyes at her daughter. "What did you do to them?"

"I didn't do anything to them! Aren't they in your room?"

"No, they're not, and they haven't touched their food. They're gone, Marge."

Marge gulped and brought a distraught hand to her throat. "Maybe they're next door?"

"We closed up the house, remember? Even the pet flap?"

Marge nodded. Unlike Tex she knew the ins and outs of their small flock of cats better than anyone, and knew this was highly unusual behavior indeed. Just then, Gran's phone rang again and she took it out of the pocket of her dressing gown. "What do you want?" she snapped.

"I just remembered something," said Odelia, for it was her. "You called me in the middle of the night, remember? Something about the cats wanting to know why they were snipped?"

Gran frowned as she threw her mind back. She hated to admit it, but it wasn't as sharp a tool as it once had been. "Oh, that's right," she said now. "They were pretty pissed off, too. Accused you of violating their feline rights or something."

"Could it be that they ran away, just to teach us a lesson?"

"Could be," Gran admitted. "In which case this is your fault. Not mine." It was never too soon to start building a defense strategy, just in case her granddaughter accused her of neglect. "I didn't do this," she added, so there could be no misunderstanding. "You did, with your unconscionable behavior."

"Everybody neuters their cats! It's the law."

"Who cares about the law? You should never have gone ahead and done it without their express consent in writing— in triplicate, preferably witnessed by the mayor *and* the governor. What if they sue? Have you thought about that?"

"Just get them back, will you? And tell them we did it for their own good."

"Fat lot of good that's going to do you now," Gran grumbled.

She disconnected again and started for the door.

"Wait—what's going on?" asked Marge.

"The cats are pissed off because they were neutralized," said Gran.

"Neutralized? Oh, you mean neutered."

"Whatever. They feel like we trampled all over their feline rights and they're probably going to the United Nations to file a class-action lawsuit and sue us for a billion bucks. So it's vital we get them back ASAP and make sure they can't get in touch with any louche or lawyerly types."

"Cats can't sue humans," said Marge. "That's ridiculous."

"We'll see how ridiculous it is when they slam you with a subpoena and haul your ass to jail," Gran growled, and headed into her room to put on some clothes. The search party was on. "Oh, and one other thing—I'm going out to Emerald Rhone's house. There's been a murder."

"A murder!"

"Well, officially they're calling it a suicide, but you know how those Hollywood types are. They probably pumped the poor woman full of cyanide and made it look like a suicide. And if I don't get there fast, the next dead body just might be Odelia!"

$\mathcal{D}$ooley and I were still ensconced on our favorite bench, while the two lovebirds—or rather love-cats—were still loving it up in some nearby tree. Foot traffic had picked up on this side of the park, with people starting to emerge from their houses, carrying briefcases and purses and getting into cars to start their working day. Dooley and I watched the steady stream of people and Dooley sighed, "Where are they all going, Max?"

"To work, and school, and shopping—who knows. Humans are very busy people. They always got something going on."

"That's probably why they get all kinds of diseases and need to go to the doctor all the time," he said wisely.

It's true. Humans go the doctor, like, all the time. Us cats don't want to be seen dead at the doctor—okay, so maybe that's a weird way of putting it but you catch my drift, right? We live far healthier, peaceful lives. When we want to sleep, we sleep. When we want to eat, we eat. And apart from that, and a few bathroom breaks and some grooming, we just relax and have a good time.

"Of course there's the fact that humans have to build all of those big houses and have to pay to keep them up," I said. "And big houses cost money."

"And clothes," Dooley said. "Humans wear all these different clothes."

"And shampoo and soap and all kinds of cosmetics," I added. "Don't forget about cosmetics."

Nope. Cats don't need to take showers or wear clothes or use hair gel. We don't even wear shoes or anything. Just a lick and a flick and we're good to go.

"Still," said Dooley. "It's nice to share those houses with our humans—those big houses they pay so much money and work so hard for."

"Yeah, sure is nice to have a place to call home," I agreed.

Which brought us right back to the reason we were languishing out there in the first place: what was taking our humans so long to organize a search and rescue party? By now they should have alerted the National Guard, or maybe the army or FBI, and launched a nationwide dragnet. Instead, crickets.

Talking about crickets, two cats deftly came walking up and joined us on the bench.

"And? All differences settled?" I asked when Brutus and Harriet huddled close together, loving smiles on their respective faces.

"I've decided to stay male," said Brutus proudly. "It kinda suits me, being male, and Harriet agrees. Isn't that right, lemon drop?"

"Exactly right, love nugget. And since I kinda like being a female, I think it works out nicely for both of us."

"Now all I need to do is convince Odelia to remove this knot from my tubes and I'll be right as rain."

"And then when she removes the knot from my tubes, we can finally start that family we've been yearning for so much," said Harriet, giving her mate a loving nudge with her head.

In actual fact Harriet had only started yearning for a family since Brutus started having doubts about his inner male or female, but I wasn't one to quibble—or start a fight with Harriet.

"What's all this about knots in tubes?" asked Dooley, interested.

"Oh, we just met Milo," said Harriet. "Remember Milo?"

How could I forget. Our neighbor's cat had lived with us for a while, and I still shivered at the recollection.

"So we got to talking about this neutering and spaying thing. And Milo told us the procedure can easily be reversed. See, they tie a knot in certain reproductive tubes—I'm not going to bore you with the details—but the important thing is that they can always untie these knots and get everything back on track. It's a simple procedure and will put us both back in business." She chuckled in a low, husky voice, indicating what she meant by business.

It went right over Dooley's head. "Reproductive tubes?" he asked. "What are reproductive tubes?"

"Oh, it's how babies are made," said Harriet. Too late she saw me gesturing wildly. Dooley hadn't yet reached the age where he'd learned about the birds and the bees, and I wasn't prepared to be the one to have to explain it to him.

"Babies?" Dooley asked, confused. "But I thought big birds brought babies into this world? What are they called? Storks?"

"That's right," I said. "Big storks live in a stork colony in the sky and they bring all the babies into this world. Isn't that right, Harriet?"

"But what about the knots and the tubes and stuff?" asked Dooley, who might look like a fool some of the time but wasn't fooled all of the time.

"Don't listen to Harriet," I said. "She's getting certain things completely mixed up. Right? *Harriet?*"

"Yeah, I'm so sorry, Dooley," she said, thunking her head in an exaggerated fashion. "I was talking about plumbing, not babies. When tubes get clogged humans send for a plumber, so that's what I was talking about. Babies are obviously brought by those nice and friendly storks. Our dear, dear friends."

"No, they're not," said Brutus, who wasn't aware of our policy to protect Dooley from some of the more graphic facts of life. "Babies are made when a male and female mate, which is why we need our tubes untied, and quick, too."

Dooley looked from Brutus to me, unsure who to believe.

"Now you've done it," said Harriet, giving her boyfriend a shove.

"Now I've done what?"

"Dooley hasn't had the talk," she hissed.

"What talk?"

"About the birds and the bees!"

"What birds? What bees?" asked Dooley.

"Well, the birds are obviously the storks I was telling you about," I said.

"And the bees? How do they feature into the thing?" asked Brutus, who was also interested. Apparently he hadn't had this particular talk yet either.

But before I could get into the matter in more detail, a sight for sore eyes suddenly materialized before us. It was Gran, and she was smiling down on us with all the benevolence of a nurturing little mother.

"Well, there you are," she said, taking a seat on the bench. "I was wondering where you went off to. There's been an emergency, my sweet and precious darlings. Your human needs you. But first tell me all about why you decided to run off and scare me half to death."

# CHAPTER 18

*W*e were in grandma's Peugeot. Well, actually not grandma's but Tex and Marge's old red Peugeot. How she ever induced them to let her drive it I do not know, for Gran is a terrible driver. Fortunately for my peace of mind I'd rarely had to endure her driving style, as usually Odelia is the one driving us around, but this time there was no escape.

"So tell me the whole story," she said as she sat hunched over the wheel, intensely scowling at the windshield as if it had personally offended her.

The car was swerving across the road, as Gran has trouble driving in a straight line, but that wasn't even the worst of it. From time to time, as I told my story and told it well, she glanced over in my direction, and took her eyes off the road. Luckily people in Hampton Cove are familiar with the Chief of Police's mother's driving, and know to jump out of the way when they see her coming. Problem is the tourists. They are innocents likely to be mowed down, like corn before Gran's sickle, and how she's managed to live this long without committing vehicular manslaughter is actually quite beyond me.

"It all began when Brutus decided he wanted to be a woman," I said.

"I have changed my mind since then," Brutus said, instigated by a poke in the ribs from a grateful Harriet.

"A woman? Why would you want to be a woman?" asked Gran, glancing back at Brutus.

"Use the rearview mirror, Gran," I suggested.

"He saw a documentary," Harriet explained.

"Yeah, that'll do it," grunted Gran. "I remember this one time I saw a documentary on drag queens. And wouldn't you know it, next day I found myself dressing up like a drag queen and parading along Main Street before I happened to catch my reflection in the barber store window and came to my senses."

"Aren't drag queens men who dress up like women?" I asked, confused.

"So? Why should men have all the fun?" Gran demanded heatedly.

"Anyway," I said, "since Brutus seemed confused about his male identity, I thought he should probably see a shrink. Seek professional help, you know."

"I get it," said Gran. "You called RuPaul."

"Who's RuPaul?"

"He's probably the cat shrink we've been looking for," said Dooley.

"But since we didn't have RuPaul's number," I continued, trying to get back to my story, "we talked to Kingman instead."

"Is he a shrink?" asked Gran, interested.

"No, but he knows every cat in Hampton Cove and probably a few in the surrounding towns, too. In the course of our conversation, Harriet revealed her main objection against Brutus becoming a female: she wants to start a family, a dream she's always harbored." Though in secret, apparently.

"A dream I've always harbored," Harriet echoed, cuddling up to Brutus, who purred contentedly. "And now it's finally happening, papa bear."

"Finally, mama bear."

"But then Kingman said no way could Harriet and Brutus start a family, as we've all been neutered—or spayed—or whatever the correct vernacular."

"Yeah, I'm with you so far," said Gran. "And that's when you rushed home and woke me up from my beauty sleep. So what made you run off and go into hiding?"

I straightened. The job of being spokesperson for an entire crew of cats is a responsible one, and I wanted to get this exactly right.

"You shouldn't have done it, Gran," said Harriet, interrupting my carefully prepared speech. "You had no right!"

"Which is exactly what I told Odelia," said Gran, nodding. She cut me a quick sideways glance. "So have you lawyered up yet?"

"Lawyered up?" I asked.

"Good. A load off my mind. Don't," she said. "Lawyer up, I mean. This is not a case you're likely to win. I mean, I know this is against your feline rights and all that jazz, but humans have rights too, or at least that's what Marge told me. And one of them is the right not to have your entire house urinated on."

"We don't urinate indoors!" I said, utterly shocked.

"No, we are civilized cats, Gran," said Dooley. "We only urinate in the designated spot, which just so happens to be covered in nice-smelling, dust-free, clumping, non-tracking, hypoallergenic cat litter for our convenience."

"I know, I know, but allegedly non-neutered cats urinate

all over the damn place, which is probably what Odelia was trying to avoid—hence the snip."

"At any rate, we want you to take us to Vena and have the procedure reversed," said Harriet. "Brutus and I are in love, and we want to start a family together to celebrate that love. Isn't that right, my cuddly lion?"

"Absolutely, sugar cookie."

Gran darted a quick look in the rearview mirror. "Start a family, huh?"

"We were thinking, maybe two or three?"

"I could go for four or five," Brutus indicated proudly.

"Oh, Super Cat."

"Oh, Wonder Cat."

"Oh, hell," Dooley muttered.

"Reverse the procedure, huh? Yeah, well, let's talk to Odelia first," said Gran, who was shuffling uncomfortably in her seat.

"Don't tell me, the procedure can't be reversed, right?" I said, feeling the way the wind was blowing.

"I didn't say that. Did I say that? I'm not a vet, so how the hell should I know? Let's talk to Odelia and that's my final word on the matter."

"So what's this about Odelia needing our help?" I asked.

"Yeah, some ditzy dame got whacked, and Odelia needs you to do that thing that you do so well."

"Snoop around for possible clues, you mean?"

"That's the one. Meanwhile I'm going to network." She sneezed, and almost ran down two old ladies who were crossing the road arm in arm.

"Network?" I asked.

"I never told anyone this, but I always wanted to be an actress," she said now, a wistful look coming over her face.

We all sat stunned. This was the first we'd ever heard of Gran's ambition.

She straightened her shoulders. "So I'm going to ask this Emerald person to give me a part in her next movie. That should launch me in the biz, don't you think?"

"Yeah, that should do it," I agreed.

Though I had a feeling Emerald might not be open to the idea as much as Gran seemed to think. The thing is, Gran is a woman with a million different projects and ideas, and as soon as she's failed at one, she immediately adopts another. I have to hand it to her, though, what she lacks in talent, she makes up for in sheer tenacity. Even though she doesn't have any discernible skill other than to create trouble for those around her, she's determined and will do whatever it takes to fulfill her ambitions, as harebrained as they might be.

"I think you'll do great, Gran," said Harriet, who was in great spirits now that her own dream of being a mom was within her grasp.

"Of course I'll do great. I see myself in the same pantheon as some of the greats of old. Greta Garbo. Bette Davis. Katharine Hepburn. Classic beauties bursting with talent. Trust me, kids, nothing in this world is free. So when you have a dream, you gotta grab it and hold on tight and never let go!"

And with this piece of advice she sneezed again, and practically ran over Father Reilly, who shook his fist and hurled a stream of classic obscenities our way.

# CHAPTER 19

*A*ll the guests had been gathered in the library, where they would be interviewed by the police officers Uncle Alec had brought in. It was just a routine thing, and yet everyone was on edge and nerves were stretched taut.

Alina, especially, looked as if she was about to have a nervous breakdown. Her face had gone deathly pale, and she was visibly shaking. Odelia, who'd opted to remain with the other guests, wondered if she should tell Alina this was merely a routine investigation, as Kimberlee's death was very obviously a suicide and would soon be deemed just that.

She approached the woman. "Are you all right?" she asked now.

Alina shook her head. "I did this," she whispered. "I did this to her. If I hadn't said those horrible things—or tried to whack her over the head with a croquet mallet, she might still be alive."

"You don't know that," said Odelia. "No one carries cyanide around unless it's for a good reason. Kimberlee must have been planning this long before she came here."

Alina seemed to awake from her stupor at these words.

"Cyanide. That's right. Reinhart said the same thing." She brought her slender fingers to her suspiciously wrinkle-free forehead. "Oh, my God. I can't even begin to contemplate what must have been going through that poor woman's mind."

"Yeah, I've been wondering about that myself," said Odelia. "So you see? There's no need to blame yourself. This had nothing to do with that fight."

Alina lowered her hand and fixed those remarkable green eyes on Odelia. They were now lined with tiny red veins. "Are you quite sure, Miss Poole?"

"I am. Like I said, she must have planned this a long time ago. Cyanide is not an easy substance to get your hands on, and—"

"Would you say she suffered a painful death?"

"Very painful, and very quick. Cyanide is what Cold War spies used to take when they were captured on enemy soil. They had it tucked into a tooth or hidden in a capsule. Then they'd bite down on the capsule or the tooth and the cyanide would do its deadly work. Hitler used one to kill himself."

Alina had been listening attentively throughout, and now displayed a tiny smile. "Amazing how much you know about the subject, Miss Poole. But then I guess reporters must have extensive knowledge of a variety of topics, right?"

"I just read about it on Wikipedia just now," said Odelia modestly.

Alina's expression hardened. "Why is it, you think, that the police are keeping us in here? Or do they think Kimberlee was murdered?"

"Oh, no, nothing like that. It's just routine—they want to find out as much as they can about the circumstances of the poor woman's death. Once they've wrapped up the investigation, they'll remove the body and—"

"Remove the body," Alina interrupted. "How perfectly horrible."

Emerald, who'd been sitting nearby, chimed in, "This is a nightmare. This weekend should have been about the celebration of friendship, but instead it's been marred by fighting and bickering and now this—I don't think I'll ever do another one of these weekends ever again."

"You know?" said Alina suddenly. "I think she did it on purpose."

"Did what on purpose?" asked Emerald as she took a swig from her Coke Emerald. Judging from the way she was slurring her words a little, Odelia had the impression it contained more than just Coca Cola.

"She chose this weekend to kill herself—so she could tarnish your reputation by her suicide. Don't you see? People will never accept this as a suicide—you know what they're like. This is going to bite you in the ass, Emerald. It's going to haunt you forever. And that's exactly what she wanted."

"The witch!" Emerald spat, shocking Odelia.

"She was a witch," Alina said. "First getting it on with my husband, now killing herself to get back at you. You should never have invited her."

"I had no choice. She was part of the cast. I couldn't very well invite everyone and not her—there would have been a scandal. She would have made such a terrible stink."

"Well, she sure made a stink now."

"Yeah, she did," Emerald agreed.

Abbey had joined them, while the husbands were all gathered by the window, talking in hushed tones. Verna, meanwhile, sat all by herself, rocking back and forth, and clearly brooding on something.

"We were just discussing how Kimberlee probably did this to try and destroy Emerald," said Alina. "I mean, why else would she kill herself here? Now? This weekend? She could have killed herself any time, any place, but she chose to do it here and now. Why? To damage poor Emerald's reputation."

"Poor Emerald's reputation," Emerald said, swirling the contents of her Coke. "A reputation now royally screwed. Fifty-year career? Poof. Gone. Because of one spiteful little cow."

"I think it's a good thing she's gone," said Abbey. "I mean," she quickly added when the others all stared at her, "I know this is a very politically incorrect thing to say and all, but you're absolutely right, Emerald. Kimberlee *was* a spiteful cow, and she deserved to die, if you'll pardon my French."

"Pardoned," Emerald said, producing a little hiccup.

"Don't you think you're being a little harsh?" asked Odelia.

Alina turned to her as if seeing her for the first time. "I'm sorry, but you didn't even know the woman. So maybe she deserves to be treated harshly."

"That's right, you didn't know her," said Emerald. "She was a terrible person. A great actress, but a terrible person."

"She slept with my husband," said Alina. "They've been sleeping together for months now."

"She slept with my husband, too," said Emerald sadly. "But then she probably slept with everybody's husband as far as I can tell. She was a horrible little tart, Kimberlee was. Just dreadful."

"She didn't sleep with mine," said Abbey. "I would know, wouldn't I?" she added when Alina scoffed and said, "Oh, please!"

"The only reason she didn't sleep with your husband is because she wasn't interested," said Emerald now, giving Abbey a sad look. "She told my Pete how Seger came on to her, and offered to have a quickie in her trailer. She said she wasn't into girly men like Seger, and turned him down flat."

Abbey looked shocked. "What?!"

"Yeah—so don't act like your Seger is a saint who practiced amazing restraint. He's just as big a philanderer as Pete or Reinhart."

"Well, shit," said Abbey. "She *was* a horrible little tart, wasn't she?"

"We're talking about a woman whose body is lying upstairs," said Odelia, who didn't think this conversation was appropriate. "Show some respect."

"I would show some respect if she hadn't gone after my husband," said Alina, her face now flushed.

"And mine," said Emerald, holding up her can and taking a sip.

"And mine," said Abbey. "Or actually my husband went after her."

"So did she go after Verna's husband?" asked Emerald now, turning to Verna, who still sat brooding in a corner, nursing a glass of an amber liquid that didn't look like apple juice.

"Worse," said Abbey, pressing her lips together.

"Worse? What are you talking about?" asked Alina.

Abbey shook her head, her lips still clamped together.

"Oh, come on, you can tell us," said Emerald, tugging at Abbey's sleeve. "We're all friends here—more or less. We told you our biggest, dirtiest secrets, so you can tell Verna's."

"Kimberlee did have an affair, but not with Verna's husband but with…" She darted a meaningful look at Verna. "… her."

Alina and Emerald look appropriately shocked, and so did Odelia.

"Kimberlee had an affair with Verna?"

"Yup," said Abbey. "And then she dumped her. Just like that."

"I didn't even know…" Emerald began.

"That she liked to play both sides? Oh, yes, she did. She

once came on to me, actually. We were best friends and she came on to me. Tried to kiss me and grab my boob. Can you imagine that? We were sitting there, chatting nicely and suddenly she grabbed my boob. Or both boobs. No, this is how it went down: she looked me in the eyes—deep, you know—then grabbed one boob, kissed me and grabbed the other. I was so shocked I didn't even react."

"And then you grabbed her boobs."

"I did not!"

"I remember—you used to be thick as thieves, until you weren't," said Alina, clasping her hand to her face.

"We were besties—or at least that's what I thought. And then one day she decided to take matters to the next level, or what she assumed the next level was, and when I told her in no uncertain terms I wasn't up for that kind of thing, she dumped me—froze me out completely, and started hitting on Verna. Soon they were thick as thieves, and a little more. Thieves with benefits."

"Oh, my God," said Emerald with a snort of shock.

"So that's why she's in mourning," said Alina. "She just lost her girlfriend."

"I don't think they were still together," said Abbey. "I'm sure Kimberlee moved on already. She wasn't one to linger. Hit and run kinda girl."

"But she had a boyfriend," said Odelia. "How did Zoltan feel about this whole... sleeping around thing?"

"Oh, he didn't like it," said Abbey. "Kimberlee once told me Zoltan hated it, and threatened to leave her if she didn't change her ways."

"Maybe she did, change her ways," said Emerald. "I mean, they're still together, aren't they?"

"Zoltan Falecki is a weak, weak man," said Abbey. "Amazing physical strength but a personality like a wet sock. He may have told her he was gonna leave her, but between telling and actually doing it lies a world of difference. So no, I don't think she changed her ways. And yes, I think Zoltan hated it."

"She really doesn't sound like the kind of person who would kill herself," said Odelia thoughtfully. "I mean," she added when all eyes turned to her, "people like that don't kill themselves. On the contrary. They thrive. They prosper. And they live life to the very fullest."

At least that was the impression Kimberlee had given her the night before. And that morning. She glanced over to Verna once again, and just in that moment the young woman looked over at her. Their eyes met, and Odelia was surprised to find in Verna's expression not the sadness and the grief she'd expected but a different emotion altogether: pure relief.

## CHAPTER 20

Franklin Johnson was having a rough day. Being a security guard for one of the world's most famous movie stars wasn't usually a walk in the park but this weekend had been worse than usual. Word had somehow gotten out that Emerald had invited a few of her famous friends over and the gate had been hounded by paps ever since. There were easily a dozen of them, with their cameras clicking incessantly the moment they thought they saw movement at the front door of Casa Emerald. Unfortunately the architect who'd designed the grounds had neglected to follow the advice of wiser, more experienced architects to design a curving driveway that hid the main house from view. Instead, it was a straight line to the house, a trait of the place the paps loved.

And then there was the fact that Emerald had decided to ignore Franklin's advice to install a solid steel-plate gate—impervious to lookie-loos and paps.

Sometimes it was almost as if she wanted to be photographed.

That morning, however, had suddenly seen a threefold

increase in activity at the gate. Now not only paps were there, hoping for a money shot of Emerald in her bathroom showing some skin, but serious reporters, too, asking for a comment or a quote, and three satellite vans from local news stations.

In other words, sheer pandemonium.

He'd almost neglected to admit the cop who'd driven up in a beat-up old squad car, figuring he was just a pap pretending to be a cop. He was a beefy guy, with a face only a mother could love, and looked like a character from a seventies cop show. His ID was legit, though, and after conferring with the lady of the house—or rather Pete, who handled such matters—he'd allowed the guy to pass through.

The sound of the bell alerted him another breach was being attempted, and he frowned at his monitor. A little old lady with little white curls sat in an old red Peugeot and was smiling at the camera.

"Please state your name and business," he said wearily.

"Hi, I'm a guest of Odelia Poole? I'm here to deliver the cats."

He blinked. Of all the lame excuses… It seemed like the crackpots were out in force today. "This is not Odelia Poole's house, ma'am. This is the residence of Emerald Rhone, and if you have no business here, please leave."

"You don't understand. I'm a guest of Odelia Poole, who's a guest of Emerald, so you gotta let me in. And did I mention I've brought the cats?"

Cats. What did cats have to do with anything? With a tired groan, he hoisted himself up from his office chair and walked out into the line of fire. Those creepy paps all started shooting pictures of him. Then, when they saw it was just him and not some celebrity, minor or major, they desisted and instead started hurling questions at a rapid-fire pace:

"So was it murder?"

"Can you confirm it's Kimberlee Cruz that died?"

"What happened to the body?"

"How did she die?"

"How did Miss Rhone react to the news?"

He waved them away with an annoyed grunt, and walked over to the gate. The little old lady was poking her head out of the little red car.

"Lemme in, will you?" she shouted from the other side of the gate. "My sciatica is acting up and if you don't let me in right now I'm gonna be in so much pain you're gonna have to call an ambulance."

"You're not invited, lady," he said, "so beat it."

"I *am* invited—by Odelia Poole. *The* Odelia Poole—the famous reporter."

"Yeah, yeah, yeah." He'd checked his list, and Odelia Poole was indeed on the guest list. Famous, though, she was not. At least he'd never heard of her.

"Or you can ask my son—Alec Lip. That's Chief of Police Alec Lip to you. He's in there, isn't he? And he needs my help."

The notion that a cop would need his mom's help brought a tiny smile to his lips.

"Hey, what is this? *Stop! Or My Mom Will Shoot?*" one pap quipped.

"Did the Chief forget his lunch? Did you bring his peanut-butter-and-jelly sandwich?" asked another.

The little old lady turned to the two paps and directed a look of such menace at them they quickly shut up.

It was true, though. Chief Lip was at the house at that moment, investigating what appeared to be a suicide. But that didn't mean a thing.

"Please get lost, ma'am," he said gruffly. "If you're not a cop or a guest I can't let you in."

"But my son—"

"If you want to talk to your son, I suggest you call him," he said, and started walking back to his guard shack.

"If you don't let me in right now I'm going to have him arrest you for obstruction of justice," the little old lady said, not sounding as pleasant and well-mannered as before. "And then you can explain to the judge how you impeded an ongoing investigation, you fat bozo!" she yelled.

He froze. Slurs about his weight always did much to sour his day. He swung around. "That was uncalled for, ma'am," he said. He now saw that a cat was seated in the passenger seat. It was fat and orange. Behind it, he saw three more cats. What the actual...

"I'm only saying it to get your attention," she said, now suddenly smiling sweetly again. "You're not fat, sir. In fact you're exactly the right weight for your size. Now if you'll call my son, you'll see that this has all been one big misunderstanding, and that I do, in fact, have every right to be here."

He had a feeling the woman was going to stand there forever, and block the gate, so he decided to humor her. He took his phone and called up to the house.

"Yeah, Johnson. What is it now?" said Pete.

"Some old woman claims to be the Chief of Police's mom. Says I need to let her in. She's brought cats."

"Cats?"

"Yeah, four of them, by the looks of things. She also says she's Odelia Poole's grandmother."

There was a momentary silence on the other end while Pete processed this, then a curt, "Hold on." Moments later, he was back. "Just let her in."

"Oh, for crying out loud," he muttered, and walked back into his shack and punched the button that operated the gate. It noiselessly swung open on its hinges. The paps all moved forward like a pack of rabid dogs, so he walked back out, his hand on his truncheon, and gave them his best menacing glare. "Back off!" he yelled. "Back off, you bunch of frickin' vultures!"

He shouldn't have bothered. The little old lady had gotten back in her car, stomped on the gas, and the car practically ran over the paps, then zoomed up the drive, pelting them all with gravel, and almost hitting a small stone statue dedicated to one of Emerald's dogs that had passed away.

"Chief's mother, my foot," Franklin muttered, and punched the button again to close the gate. This time he hoped a pap would be dumb enough to get his head stuck between it, or his butt up on the spikes, but no such luck. Instead they all stayed on their side of the gate and so the long day wore on.

# CHAPTER 21

*C*hase stuck his head in the door and announced, "Your cats are here."

"What?" said Odelia, getting up.

"And your grandmother."

"Wait, what?" she said, hurrying to the door.

Chase led her out into the hallway, where they arrived just in time to see Marge's old Peugeot drive up and disgorge one little old lady and four cats.

"You've got to be kidding me," said Odelia in a low voice.

"Hey, I didn't invite them, and neither did your uncle, which means you did, right?"

They shared a look, and Chase's face took on a grim expression. "She invited herself."

"Of course she did."

"Only your grandmother would invite herself and four cats to the house of the greatest living acting legend and think she can get away with it."

Behind them, Emerald had materialized. "Who is that woman?" she asked now. "And are those… cats?!"

"That's my grandmother," Odelia announced blithely, "and she's brought my cats."

Emerald looked stricken, but not furious. Still under the impact of the recent tragedy that had befallen her. "You know I'm allergic to cats, right? I strictly told you over the phone not to bring cats into my home."

"I know," said Odelia. "But my grandmother has a way of inserting herself into places without asking for permission first."

"And I can see why. It's very hard for any homeowner to throw a little old lady out on the street."

"So she can stay?"

"I don't know," said Emerald, shaking her head. "My allergies…"

"Oh, but I'll keep the cats far away from you," said Odelia, even though she didn't believe for one second that Emerald was actually allergic to cats.

"They're not very allergy-inducing," Chase said helpfully.

Emerald stared at him for a moment, then said sweetly, "For a cop you're not very bright, are you, Mr. Kingsley?"

It was probably the first time Chase had ever been called stupid, but he took it well. "I'm sorry, ma'am. It's just that—"

"All right," said Emerald, throwing up her hands. "I guess if I'm going to put with a horde of cops in my house, I might as well accept their cats along with them. Though I always had the impression cops favored dogs. But then what do I know?" And she stalked off, only to be replaced by her husband, who looked even more nervous than usual.

"About those cats…" he said.

"It's fine, Pete," said Emerald, walking away. "I dealt with it."

"But you're allergic to cats, my pet," said Pete.

"I've dealt with it—now you deal with it!" she shouted,

and husband and wife returned to the library, slamming the door as they did.

Odelia watched on as her grandmother returned to the car, started the engine and parked it a few inches more to the right, almost clipping a nice marble statue of a dog with the rear fender. She got out and trudged up the steps.

Odelia met her halfway. "Gran! Didn't I tell you not to come?!"

"Now is that the way to greet your beloved grandmother?" She looked around the marble entrance hall. "So this is how the other half lives, huh? Oh, hi, Chase. Didn't know you were here, too."

"I'm Odelia's plus-one," said Chase.

"Of course you are. There was a time I was her plus-one, but you managed to usurp me. Not that I blame her. If I had to choose between a hot young stud and a feeble old lady with one foot in the grave I wouldn't hesitate."

"Oh, hey, you guys," said Odelia, crouching down and greeting her cats.

"We finally made it," said Max, looking shaken. "For a moment there I thought we'd all end up in a ditch." He leaned closer and dropped his voice to a whisper. "Your grandmother can't drive."

"I heard that!" said Gran who, in spite of her status as a feeble old lady with one foot in the grave, had remarkable eyesight and hearing.

"What did you hear?" asked Chase, who'd heard nothing.

"Nothing," said Gran, then handed Chase a bulky suitcase. "Bring this up to my room, will you? Make yourself useful for a change."

Chase stared bemusedly at the suitcase, then said, "Yes, ma'am," and was off in the direction of the staircase.

"So where's the dead broad?" asked Gran.

"Upstairs—don't tell me you're here to investigate the suicide," said Odelia.

"Suicide? Murder, you mean."

"Pretty sure it's suicide."

Gran patted her cheek. "You're so naive. Now show me the dead woman. I'm gonna nail this perp before the body is cold or my name isn't Vesta the Great."

"Your name isn't Vesta the Great."

"That's what I said." She suddenly caught sight of a young police officer and collared him. "Hey, you! Show me the body!"

"Yes, ma'am," said the officer, recognizing his boss's mother, and graciously took her arm and led her up the stairs.

&.

"Oh, boy," I said, as I watched Gran disappear from view.

"You guys better follow me to my room," said Odelia. "Emerald is allegedly allergic to cats, and doesn't want you skulking around."

"If you didn't want us skulking around you shouldn't have brought us here," said Harriet, who wasn't used to being hidden away like a stowaway.

"I didn't bring you—Gran did," said Odelia.

"What? We thought this was your idea," I said.

"No, it wasn't. I told her not to come."

"You told us not to come?" asked Dooley. "You don't want us here?"

"I didn't say that!"

"You literally just did," said Harriet dryly.

"Let's go up to my room," said Odelia, who looked uncomfortable.

She led the way up the stairs, the four of us following in her wake.

As we arrived upstairs, a little white fluffy dog greeted us.

"And who are you?" asked the dog, not very welcoming, I thought.

"Oh, hey, Fanny," said Odelia, crouching down. Turning to us, she added, "You guys, meet Fanny. She's Emerald's. Isn't that right, Fanny?"

Fanny ignored Odelia, her attention fixed on us—the intruders. "I should probably tell you cats are not allowed in this house. We are allergic to cats."

"Give me a break," said Brutus. "A dog allergic to cats? What a bunch of—"

"I didn't say *I* was allergic to cats," said Fanny, tilting her chin. "I said *we* are allergic to cats—in reference to my beloved human Emerald."

"Well, I guess she'll just have to get used to us," said Harriet, who had no patience for uppity little doggies—or uppity humans, for that matter.

"I can't say it any clearer than this," said Fanny, who wasn't budging. She assumed a fighting position, which was a little funny for a teensy weensy ball of fluff. "You shall not pass!"

Harriet rolled her eyes. "Who died and made you queen of the mansion?"

"Died?" Fanny cocked a whisker at Harriet. "Who told you someone died?"

"Gran did. And she's here to solve the murder."

"Murder!" Fanny cried. "Nobody told me about no murder."

"That's because there was no murder," I said.

"Wait, does she think it was murder?" asked Odelia, crouching down.

Fanny stared from Harriet to Odelia. "Can you... talk to your human?"

"Yes, I can," said Harriet triumphantly. "And she can talk to us, too."

"That's more or less a given," I murmured.

"Ask her if she saw what happened," said Odelia.

"I wasn't there," said Fanny. "But I know someone who was. Stevie."

"Who's Stevie?" asked Harriet.

"The dead woman's Brussels Griffon. She was in the room with her."

"We have to talk to Stevie," said Harriet, looking up at Odelia. "She was there when the dead woman died."

Odelia smiled and patted Harriet's head. "Well, done, honey. We'll do that later. First I'll show you your room. Oh, and before I forget, did Gran bring your stuff?"

"I'll bet she forgot," I said.

"No worries," said Odelia. "I'll borrow one of Fanny's bowls."

"Hey—no borrowing my bowls!" yelled Fanny. "I need all of them!"

But we'd already reached Odelia's room and she now ushered us in.

The moment she'd closed the door, I turned to her. "All right. Let's get this out of the way once and for all. Why did you have a vital part of our anatomy removed for no good reason at all?"

## CHAPTER 22

"Look, I'm sorry I never told you," said Odelia, which was a good way to start, I thought, "but it was for your own good," which I thought was a bad way to finish.

"For our own good?!" cried Harriet. "You took away our proactive capacity. How can that be for our own good?"

"Reproductive," I corrected her.

"Whatever!"

"Look, before we get into this, I want you to know this hasn't affected you in any way—on the contrary, it's been proven that male cats that are neutered suffer less risk of disease and certain cancers, and the same goes for females. It also limits aggression in males and the mating instinct in females."

Looked like it hadn't worked for Harriet, I thought, who had a very powerful mating instinct. And as far as aggression in males went, Brutus could be just a touch too aggressive in my view. But who was I to contradict Odelia's words? She seemed to know all about the topic—more than us cats!

"So you see?" Odelia concluded her instructional little talk. "It's all good!"

"The thing is, Odelia," said Brutus, "that Harriet and I want to start a family. You know, settle down, raise a couple of rug rats. So we'd like very much for you to make an appointment with Vena and get these tubes untied."

"Yeah, we've decided to take our relationship to the next level," said Harriet, "and bless the love we share with offspring of our own."

"Um... the thing is, I'm afraid that's not possible," said Odelia.

"How do you mean? Tied tubes can be untied," said Harriet. "It's a minor procedure, or so Milo told us. Just like untying shoelaces."

"You do know that Milo is a serial liar and a fantasist, right?"

"Of course I know," said Harriet. "But he wouldn't lie about a thing like that. We're talking about the sanctity of feline life here. He wouldn't mess with that."

"Of course he would," I said. "It's Milo. Nothing is sacred or off-limits."

"But how about the tubes and stuff?" asked Harriet.

"I still don't get the whole tube thing," said Dooley in an aside to me.

"We'll discuss it later," I said.

"And the birds and the bees and the storks, too?"

"Promise," I whispered, mentally adding the tube thing to the list.

"The thing is..." said Odelia, but then the door swung open and Uncle Alec walked in, followed by Chase and Gran, in that order.

Ugh. Looked like Odelia had been saved by the bell.

"Nasty business," Uncle Alec said as he took a seat on a

nice overstuffed chair. It creaked dangerously in protest. "Bad way to go for that poor girl."

"Yeah, if I were to take my own life, I wouldn't take cyanide, that's for sure," said Gran.

"So did you talk to everybody?" asked Odelia.

"We did. From what I can gather Kimberlee wasn't well-liked, especially amongst the women. The men, though, gave me a completely different story. They were all nuts about her, except Verna Rectrix's husband, who hated her."

"I think I know why," said Odelia. "Kimberlee had an affair with Verna."

"Yeah, I can see how a husband wouldn't like that," said Uncle Alec. "But he also told me Kimberlee did drugs, and tried to involve Verna."

Odelia blinked. "That's a new one. Kimberlee was a drug addict?"

"According to him she liked to snort a line of coke from time to time, and wasn't averse to a bit of smack. And since she and Verna were having an affair, it was the husband's fear she was introducing Verna to the same lifestyle."

"And was she?"

"Verna claims she refused to partake in that aspect of her girlfriend's life. But she admitted she was smitten with her, and had been thinking about getting a divorce and getting together with Kimberlee for real."

"And did Kimberlee feel the same way?"

"According to the boyfriend she did not. He claims she just liked playing the field. Being young and happy in Hollywood meant she liked to indulge in all the vices she hadn't had access to in her home state of Colorado. He also felt she would have settled down eventually and left this self-destructive path behind once she was a little further along in her career."

"So who do you think did it?" asked Gran as she studied a

portrait of Emerald that decorated the wall. It depicted the Queen of Hollywood in a long, bedazzled white gown, holding aloft one of her many Oscars.

"Did what?"

"Killed her."

"No one killed her, Ma," said Alec. "She killed herself, remember?"

"I'm not stupid, Alec. Obviously a woman on the cusp of a great career is not going to kill herself. And definitely not with cyanide, which made her beautiful face look really ugly and ruined her shot at an open casket, unless the mortician is a magician who can work a miracle, which I honestly doubt."

"Look, the room was locked from the inside, and there's no sign anyone tampered with that can of Coke. No, this is suicide, plain and simple."

"But why? Why would she do it?"

"Who cares? She did it—end of story." He got up. "Now please don't get carried away and start thinking this is some kind of murder mystery, okay? I'm filing my report and I'm calling it suicide."

"So where did she get the cyanide?" asked Gran, who wasn't one to let something like this go just because her son said so.

"Chase is checking into that. Chase?"

"Kimberlee was in a lot of different productions the last couple of years," said Chase. "Also overseas. It's not inconceivable she got her hands on a small stash of cyanide while filming in Europe, or even Russia, where she played Anastasia in a miniseries last year."

"The same goes for all of these ladies," said Gran. "Emerald, Abbey, Alina and Verna. They all filmed overseas, and they all could have come into the possession of cyanide."

"But why would they kill her?" asked Alec.

"Why not? They're all rivals. I mean, didn't you watch *Big*

*Little Secrets*? Those women may have looked like friends, but anyone with the slightest knowledge of human nature could tell they were really rivals deep down."

"There was a lot of hatred directed at Kimberlee," Odelia admitted. "Alina hated her for having an affair with her husband. Emerald, same story. Verna had been dumped and wasn't taking it well. And Abbey used to be best friends with her until they had a falling-out and Abbey was ghosted. There was no love lost between these women. Quite the contrary, in fact."

"So basically you're saying one of them entered the room, made Kimberlee drink a cyanide-laced can of Coke, then walked out again, making sure the room was locked from the inside?"

Odelia stared at her gran, who nodded. "I'm not sure," she admitted.

"Reasonable doubt," Chase said. "You have to admit something smells fishy, Chief. And I'm not talking about the smell of cyanide."

The Chief raked his fingers through his few remaining hairs. "Okay, so I would have preferred if she took a bunch of sleeping pills or maybe even used one of her silk scarves, but that doesn't mean she didn't do it."

"She looked fine to me," said Odelia. "Before she stormed off and went up to her room? She didn't strike me as a woman about to commit suicide."

The Chief eyed her for a moment, then finally nodded. "Okay, so convince me. Make me see the light."

Odelia smiled. "You have to give us time, Uncle Alec."

"You have twenty-four hours, and then I'm calling it. All right?" Before he left, he wagged his finger in his mother's face. "And you, better behave, okay? I don't want any complaints."

"When have I ever not behaved?" said Gran indignantly.

"Oh, heaven help me," said the Chief, and left the room.

"This is so great!" Gran cried. "The gang is back together!"

The gang had never been apart, I thought. Except for a brief interlude last night. And while Odelia, Chase and Gran sat down to compare notes, suddenly a voice piped up. It was Harriet.

"So are you seriously telling me Brutus and I can't start a family?!!!!"

# CHAPTER 23

"*Y*ou do realize that a single female feline and her litter can produce offspring totaling 370.000 in a seven-year period, right?" said Gran.

"Holy cow," I said. "Half a million kittens? That's a nice, big family."

"We don't want half a million kittens, though, right, snuggle pooh?" said Brutus, as he cast a nervous glance at his one true love.

"No! Of course not!" said Harriet. "We'll start with just the one, then maybe have another one in a year or so—a little brother or sister."

"Look, toots, this is crazy talk," said Gran. "Cats don't get to choose the number of kittens they're going to have. Expect between two and five in your first litter. And seeing as cats are in heat several times a year, multiply that number by three. Plus, do you really think Brutus is the only one who'll come sniffing at your butt once you're in heat? Forget it! Every cat on the block will be all over you. You won't be able to fend those suckers off!"

"See, that's why we did this," said Odelia, sitting down

next to Harriet. "We wanted to save you the inconvenience of being in heat all the time, and being pregnant all the time. It's not the happy home you expect it to be, Harriet. Cats are not people."

"Tell me about it," I said. "Half a million kittens."

Brutus was now looking distinctly ill at ease. The thought of fathering half a million babies seemed to have him discombobulated.

"I don't get it," said Dooley. "What's all this talk about being in heat?"

"It's when a female cat is ready to, um, be with a male cat," said Gran.

"But Harriet is ready to be with Brutus all the time. Does that mean she's in heat all the time?"

We all chuckled softly at this. Dooley wasn't wrong.

"Wow, wow, wow!" Chase suddenly cried. "What the hell is going on here?!"

Oops. Looked like Odelia and Gran had totally forgotten Chase was in the room.

"Oh, we were just fooling around, me and Gran," said Odelia, trying to project an air of happy unflappability and doing a pretty good job at it.

"You were talking to your cats! And they were responding! I could see their little mouths moving, and how you were actually... talking! And they were talking back!"

"Don't be silly, Chase," said Odelia. "Nobody talks to cats. That's crazy."

"I know! It is crazy—but it just happened! I saw it!"

"Oh, Chase..."

"And it's not the first time. This has happened before!"

"I think the jig is up," said Gran. "I think it's time to level with him."

"Level with me about what?" asked Chase.

Odelia looked doubtful. "Are you sure?"

"Yes, I do."

Odelia studied her grandmother for a moment, then nodded pensively.

"Sit down, hun," Gran told Chase. "This might come as something of a shock to you."

Chase sat down, looking a little apprehensive. "What's going on?"

"The thing is, Odelia and her mom and me? We can all talk to cats."

Chase waited, then when nothing more came, said suspiciously, "This is a joke, right? This is some kind of trick you're pulling on me."

"No joke," said Odelia. "And Gran is right. It's time you finally learned the truth. You've been suspecting it for a long time, and we always managed to convince you you were seeing things. Well, you were right the whole time. We really can talk to cats, and they can really understand us and talk back."

"Well, duh," I said. "If he hasn't gotten the message by now he hasn't been paying attention."

"He got it a while back, though," said Dooley. "Remember how he talked to us when we were all sitting on the porch swing?"

"Yeah, and he still managed to convince himself he was seeing things."

"What are they saying?!" asked Chase.

"They're saying they thought you figured it out a while back—particularly that one time when you were out on the porch and you interrogated them."

"They understood what I was saying? But this is incredible!"

"Yeah, it is kinda incredible," said Odelia with a smile. "The thing is—no one can know, Chase. Which is why I didn't want to tell you until... Well, until I was…"

133

"Until she knew you were the real deal," said Gran, finishing Odelia's sentence.

Chase glanced up at Odelia. "I'm the real deal?"

She nodded a little coyly.

He stared at me for a moment, then said, "Translate this for me, will you? What kind of underwear was I wearing yesterday morning?"

"No need to translate," said Odelia. "They can understand us humans pretty well. Max?"

"Is this a trick question? Dancing blue mice on a pink background."

"Dancing blue mice on a pink background," said Odelia.

"Oh, my God," said Chase with a grin of surprise. "He's the only one who saw me, so it must be true."

"Of course it's true, you numbnuts," said Gran. "Do you think we'd be lying about a thing like that? Now get with the program or remove yourself from the room already, would you?"

"Oh, I'm staying put," he said, still staring at me. "Amazing. I mean, I had my suspicions, but…" He looked up. "Does Tex know?"

"Of course. Dad has known for years. And so does Uncle Alec. They're the only ones, though."

"My husband didn't know—I never felt like telling him," said Gran. "And he wouldn't have believed me anyway. But then he was a jackass."

"Can I… learn the language?" asked Chase.

Odelia shook her head. "It's not so much about language than about some sort of mystical connection. Only the women in our family have the gift."

"Yeah, Alec doesn't have it," Gran confirmed. "Though he claims he can talk to goats. Easy for him to say. I've never seen a goat in Hampton Cove."

"Alec can talk to goats?" asked Chase.

"I think he was pulling my leg." She clapped her hands. "Now can we get going on this murder business? I want this wrapped before dinner. I don't do murder mysteries on a full stomach, and something tells me I'm going to indulge tonight."

"Okay," said Odelia. "Max, you and the others spread out and talk to as many pets as you can."

"I thought we weren't supposed to wander around?" said Harriet.

"Emerald isn't allergic, I'm sure of it," said Gran. "She didn't even sneeze once. So you wander around to your heart's content, my pet."

"Meanwhile we'll take another look at the crime scene photos," said Odelia. "Maybe there's something we overlooked."

She opened the door to let us out, and the four of us tiptoed from the room. As we moved out, Chase gave us a big thumbs-up. We gave him a paws-up in return, and then we were off to the races.

# CHAPTER 24

*I* thought our mission lacked both purpose and structure, and I said as much to the others. "I mean, it's not as if we're in downtown Hampton Cove and we can chat to Kingman and Clarice and the others and find out what the word on the street is," I said.

"This time we have to find out what the word in the castle is," said Dooley, as he glanced around this new environment admiringly.

"It's not a castle, Dooley," said Harriet. "It's just a big house."

"A castle is a big house," I said.

"Fine, whatever," said Harriet, who was clearly not in the best of moods.

"Are you all right, tootsie roll?" asked Brutus, who'd noticed the same thing.

"I don't get why humans can settle down and have a nice little family and when us cats try to do the same they sound the alarm."

"Didn't you hear Gran?" I said. "A single cat can produce offspring numbering almost half a million souls. That's a lot of mouths to feed. And where do you think those cats will end up? At the pound, being euthanized."

"What's euthanized, Max?" asked Dooley without missing a beat.

"That's nothing for you to concern yourself with, Dooley," I said.

"Euthanized is when they keep cats at the pound indefinitely," said Harriet.

"Indefinitely, as in they never get to leave the pound and find a home?"

"That's right," I said. It wasn't a lie, per se. Those cats would never leave the pound. Alive, at least. "So you see, this neutering business is the humane thing to do."

"It may be humane, but it's definitely not feline," grumbled Harriet.

"We can still adopt, sweet pea," said Brutus.

"It's not the same and you know it," Harriet said. "I'm going to ask Odelia to make an exception for me. All she needs to do is to ask Vena to untie my tube, then tie it up again when I've had my 2.4 babies. How hard can it be?"

"She also needs to untie my tube," said Brutus, who didn't seem to like the prospect of being operated on.

"So? That's a small sacrifice to make for eternal bliss and familial happiness," said Harriet, giving her mate a gentle nudge.

"Oh, all right," he said. "We'll ask Odelia once we've finished this mission." He turned to me. "What's our mission, Max?"

"Talk to all creatures great and small and report back to Odelia," I said. "Oh, and try to stay out of Emerald's way. She may or may not be allergic."

"Like Tex is allergic to Gran?" asked Dooley.

"More like how some people are allergic to pollen."

"Speaking of pollen. What's the deal with those birds and bees, Max?"

"Ugh," Harriet muttered. "Brutus, let's go. We have a mission to finish, and a very important question to ask Odelia."

Brutus dutifully followed his designated mate for life, and held up his paw in a gesture of goodbye.

"So about those birds and bees," said Dooley.

"Can we talk about that later?" I said. "We only have today to solve this murder—if that's what this is—so we need to move fast."

"Oh, all right. But you won't forget? I really want to know. And I also want to know what this business with the tubes is all about. It sounds fascinating."

I heaved a silent sigh. Why was it always me who had to have the tough conversations?

We trudged along, and already I was wondering how we were going to pull this off. In a big place like this, all participants were locked up in their rooms, not unlike the way the inhabitants of Hampton Cove were locked up in their homes. Only with homes pets were free to come and go as they pleased, thanks to the invention of the fantastic and revolutionary pet flap. And as far as I could tell there were no pet flaps in the doors on this particular second-floor hallway, which presumably was where all the pets were holed up.

"We better head down and outside, Max," said Dooley. "Sooner or later all these dogs have to go for a walk to do their business, so that's our best shot at having a crack at them."

I slowly turned to my friend. "Dooley, that's brilliant!"

"Gee, thanks, Max. The thought just occurred to me."

"And a good thing it did. See? If you don't let your mind get cluttered with useless information about birds and bees and tubes you get to put in some good thinking."

"I still want to know about the birds and the bees and the tubes, though."

"Of course you do," I said, and then we made our way down that nice marble staircase and wandered around downstairs until we managed to wend our way into a large dining room whose doors were open, a gentle breeze wafting in from outside. We'd arrived at the fabled grounds of Casa Emerald, where the dogs of the house presumably all met up to do their business, as humans euphemistically like to call the doo-doo that dogs do.

"So weird that dogs are supposed to be these ultra-smart creatures and yet they still haven't learned how to use a litter box," said Dooley, taking the words right out of my mouth.

Immediately upon our arrival we spotted our first victim. It was a Chihuahua, and it was being led on its leash by a petite blond-haired woman I recognized as Abbey Moret, star of such movies as *Blond Ambition 1* and *Blond Ambition 2: Ambitiously Blonder*. She was smoking a cigarette, staring off into the middle distance. The Chihuahua, meanwhile, sniffed around a nearby rosebush, lifted its hind leg and performed what is colloquially called a wee.

"Yuck, how disgusting," Dooley said.

The mutt looked up when he overheard us, and said, in a surprisingly deep and rumbling voice, "Watch what you say, cats."

"I wasn't saying anything," said Dooley.

"You were commenting on my sanitary break," he grumbled.

"The thing is, we would like to ask you a couple of questions. Mr. Mutt," I said in as pleasant and deferential a tone as felinely possible.

"Call me August," he said, sniffing his own wee.

"Yuck," Dooley said, and I gave him a gentle shove. No

need to antagonize what potentially might be an important witness to a potentially horrendous crime.

"So a woman died today," I began.

"Yeah, I know. Terrible business, sirs. Just terrible," said August.

"So what are your thoughts?"

The Chihuahua thought hard, judging from the way he puckered up his face. "Thoughts?" he said finally, as if surprised we assumed he had any.

"What do you think happened?"

"Well, she died, didn't she? Took some kind of poison and died."

Very enlightening. "Is that what your human thinks?" I asked, glancing up at Abbey, who was still frowning hard throughout her cigarette break.

"Yeah, that's exactly what she thinks. She also thinks it's probably good riddance, as she wasn't particularly fond of the dead woman."

"What does your master think?"

"Oh, he's a little sad. I think he liked the dead woman."

"Kimberlee," I said.

"Excuse me?"

"Her name was Kimberlee."

"It still is," said Dooley. "I mean," he added when I glanced over at him, "it's not because she's dead that suddenly she's Jane Doe or something, right?"

Dooley was on fire today! "You're absolutely right," I said with an indulgent smile. "So your master liked Kimberlee, huh?"

"Yeah, he liked her a lot. In fact Abbey just caught him studying pictures of her on his phone and crying in his beard. No idea why. Maybe he's allergic to lingerie, cause that's all she was wearing in the pictures. Pretty weird, huh?"

"So do you think he liked liked her?" I asked.

"Liked liked her?"

"Did he like her the way he likes your mistress?"

"Oh, you mean did they kiss and hug and lie on top of each and make strange noises?"

I winced at the mental image. "Yeah, exactly like that."

"I don't think so," said August, "though that's exactly what Abbey accused him of just now. They had a huge fight when she discovered him staring at those pictures. She said he was having an affair, whatever that's supposed to mean, and that's why he was so sad she was dead. And then he said she was full of crap and he cried some more. Humans, right? They're so weird."

"So did he? Have an affair with Kimberlee?"

"If Abbey said it, it must be true. She's a sharp cookie, my mistress."

"But you never saw him with Kimberlee, right?"

"Hey, man. I'm not my master's keeper. I don't know what he gets up to when I'm not around."

"One final question. This is very important, August. Do you think someone may have murdered Kimberlee? Your master, maybe? Or your mistress?"

The Chihuahua stared at me with his big brown eyes. I could tell this was a tough one. "Murdered her? But I thought she murdered herself?"

"It's possible she was murdered by someone else."

"Which is why it's called murder," Dooley explained.

"I know what murder is, cat," he said.

"So? Could Abbey or her husband have killed Kimberlee?"

"Oh, sure," said August. "Only they didn't, did they? Cause she killed herself."

Abbey gave the leash a yank. "Come along, August," she snapped. Then she saw us and frowned. "Weird," she muttered. "Now I'm seeing cats."

Then she walked off, her little doggie tripping behind her.

"See ya later, cats!" August cried, and then he was gone.

"That was a big flop," I said.

"At least we have one suspect," said Dooley. "Abbey? If her husband was having an affair with Kimberlee, she had a motive to get rid of the woman."

"Right you are, Dooley," I said. Dang it. Soon Dooley was going to become lead feline investigator, with me as his funny and slightly ridiculous sidekick!

## CHAPTER 25

$\mathcal{W}$e returned to the house, after ascertaining there were no more canine witnesses to be interviewed, and for a moment just sat there, trying to figure out our next move. Or at least I thought about our next move, while Dooley merely stared at a giant pile of Coke cans. They were called Coke Emerald, for some reason, and appeared to be some kind of special edition.

"I wonder if the Coca-Cola Company will ever make a Coke for cats," said Dooley.

"Personally I don't care for the taste," I said. "Too fizzy."

"Yeah, they should probably invent a fizzy-less Coke if they want to appeal to the feline demographic."

"Or you could open a can and leave it out for a couple of hours. That takes care of the fizziness."

We shared a glance. "Yuck," we said simultaneously.

I'd tried Coke once, when Uncle Alec, in exuberant mood, had first let me have a sip of beer—double yuck—and then a sip of Coke. Ugh. No way.

"They say Coke can turn a rusty nail into a regular nail,"

said Dooley. "So if a human has a rusty nail in his stomach, and drinks a lot of Coke, it will eventually turn into a regular nail."

"Why would a human swallow a rusty nail?"

"Beats me," said Dooley, "but that's what I heard Tex tell Marge once."

Humans. They're so weird.

We moved through the house, and up the stairs. My immediate goal was to talk to Kimberlee's dog Stevie, the one who'd been in the room with her when it happened. If anyone would know what went down, it was him.

Thinking logically, Stevie would be in the custody of Kimberlee's boyfriend, who presumably would have been given a different room. We stood at the top of the stairs and stared down the long hallway. There were a lot of rooms, and of course they all had their doors closed.

"We'll have to play this by ear," I said.

"Whose ear?" asked Dooley.

"Any ear. We need to improvise."

"Don't we always?"

We did. It's nice to be able to tell people you have some kind of plan when you're working a case, but the fact of the matter is that your true sleuth mostly relies on his gut. And since I had the largest gut, I usually got to decide.

So I put my ear against door after door, then sniffed the floor hard. You may not know this, but cats have amazing sense of smell, and hearing—a lot more powerful than any human. And that's what I was putting to work for me now: we needed to find this pooch and by golly we were going to find him.

"I think he's in here, Max," said Dooley. "I smell pooch."

"I smell pooch, too," I said. "Let the games begin."

And we both started meowing at the top of our lungs.

Anyone familiar with our capacity for yowling knows it can be both piercing and extremely annoying. It didn't take long, therefore, for the door to be yanked open and a wiry-looking human with a tan face to appear. He first looked left and then right, before finally looking down. Classic mistake. By the time he looked down, we'd already slipped between his legs and into the room.

Dooley and I spread out, in search of the mutt Stevie.

"Got him!" said Dooley from the other room.

We were in a nice-looking suite, with separate bedroom, living space and bathroom. The dog was in the bedroom, lying on a four-poster bed and looking sadly at a picture of his mistress that stood perched on the nightstand.

The wiry-looking man with the tan face, meanwhile, muttered something about morons and slammed the door shut. He never even saw us, the doofus.

"Hey there," I said as I jumped up on the bed.

"Hey yourself," said Stevie, wiping away a tear. To my surprise, Stevie was a she, and not a he. A tawny-colored Brussels Griffon with a well-groomed mustache and beard and looking at me with intelligent eyes.

"Hi," said Dooley, now also jumping up on the bed and joining us.

"Hey," said the Ewok lookalike.

"We're detectives," I said by way of introduction, "and we're investigating the possible murder of your mistress Kimberlee."

Stevie uttered a stifled sob at this. "Kimberlee. Oh, how I'm going to miss her." She directed a sad look at the framed picture and burst into tears.

"We're very sorry for your loss, by the way," said Dooley. "I can't imagine what it must be like to lose your human like that."

She gave Dooley an appreciative look. "Thanks," she said softly.

I hadn't even thought of offering my condolences. Instead I'd just barged in and was about to launch into a barrage of questions. Rude. Rude and tactless.

"She was a wonderful person," said Stevie. "The best. Hard to believe she would do this to herself. She had so much to live for. This is a sad, sad day."

"That's the thing," I said, seeing my opening. "We think she may not have done this to herself. We think she may have been murdered. And we were hoping you could help us figure out who killed her."

"You were there, right?" said Dooley.

"I was," said Stevie sadly. "I was there until the bitter end."

"So can you tell us a little bit about what happened?" I asked.

"There's not much to tell. I was in the next room, napping and dreaming of rabbits."

"Do dogs often dream of rabbits?" asked Dooley, interested.

"Not now, Dooley," I said.

"So I was lying in my basket, dreaming of rabbits and birds."

"Birds?" asked Dooley. "That's a coincidence. I dream of birds, too. Like, every night. And sometimes during the day, too. What kind of birds?"

"Dooley," I said warningly.

"So I was lying in my basket, dreaming of rabbits and birds and cats—"

Dooley opened his mouth to say something, but he caught my eye and shut up.

"Carry on," I said kindly. "You dreamed of rabbits and birds and cats and then what happened?"

"Well, then Kimberlee had a visitor. I didn't hear them

come in, only woke up when I heard voices. They were chatting about this and that—I didn't really pay attention. Humans are always gabbing on and on and you kinda lose interest after a while." She sniffed. "If only I'd paid more attention, she might still be alive."

"You don't know that."

"Yeah, you can't think that way," said Dooley.

"So they talked and then this person left, cause they stopped talking, and then there was a strange noise. Like steam escaping from a kettle. And when curiosity overcame my laziness, and I finally tripped into the other room, there she was, lying on the floor, writhing about in some sort of agony. I quickly hurried up to her, desperate to help, but she'd already stopped moving. I started yapping like crazy, hoping someone would come. Someone must have heard, for there was a tapping on the door, but of course they couldn't get in—the door was locked.

"And when I just kept on screaming and screaming and scratching the door, they broke it down. It was Zoltan, along with Pete. But by then it was too late. Zoltan tried to revive her, but Pete took one whiff at her, and pulled him back. Said he could get whatever killed her into his system, too, and collapse. They called an ambulance, but nothing could be done. She was gone."

"That's a terrible story," said Dooley compassionately. "And I'm so very, very sorry. Imagine if something like that happened to Odelia, Max?"

I didn't want to even to contemplate that scenario so I decided not to go there. "This person chatting with Kimberlee, who was it?" I asked.

"I don't know," she said sadly. "Like I said, I wasn't paying attention. I think it was a woman, though. Because of the timbre of the voice?"

"And what were they talking about?"

"I only picked up a few words. Um…" She thought hard.

"Go on," said Dooley. "Try to remember. This is very important."

"I think they discussed a project of some kind? How Kimberlee would be perfect as a director?"

"A director," I said, sharing a meaningful look with Dooley. There was only one director present at the mansion, and even though he was a man that didn't mean he wasn't the one in the room with Kimberlee.

"One thing puzzles me, though," she said. "How did this person leave the room? The door was locked from the inside. So how did they leave?"

It was a mystery that we hadn't cracked yet, but I was confident we would at some point.

We both thanked the grief-stricken doggie and moved into the other room, where Zoltan was seated in front of the television, nursing a drink, and staring at the news reports about Kimberlee's death. He sat sagged in his seat, and looked as unhappy as Stevie.

"Yoo-hoo, mister," said Dooley, but he didn't pay attention.

"Can you let us out now, please?" I asked.

No reaction. The man was completely spaced out.

"Maybe try the yowling thing again?" Dooley suggested.

"Or we could go that way," I suggested, indicating the balcony.

If Zoltan's balcony was like most balconies, it would lead to the next one, and then the next, and finally would lead us back to Odelia's room.

So we moved to the French windows, and out onto the balcony, then hopped up onto the stone balustrade and glanced around for the next balcony.

As I'd suspected, it was well within reach, and a quick

jump later we were in the next room. Loud voices drifted from inside, and I pricked up my ears to determine their source. They appeared to be a couple fighting, so we settled down on the balcony, and decided to have a listen. Feline spies at work.

# CHAPTER 26

"*I*'m done apologizing, Thaw!" the woman said. "You hear me? Done!"

"I'm not asking you to apologize, Verna," said this Thaw person. "All I want is to understand. How could you throw away this—for that!"

"I loved her," said Verna. "I really loved her and I thought she loved me."

"Well, you were obviously wrong about that, weren't you? I mean, I'm not going to say I told you so, but I did warn you. She's the kind of person who uses people. Uses them and then throws them away when she's done."

"I know—and I hated her for it."

"I thought you said you loved her?"

"I loved her and then I hated her. I still hate her—for what she did to me—to us."

"You should have thought about that sooner, Verna. It's too late now."

"But I did what you asked me to!"

"I never asked you to... Oh, God. What a mess."

There was a knock at the door and then the man stepped

out onto the balcony. He stared down at us, frowned, then said, "Huh. Cats," and proceeded to ignore us. As if we were part of the furniture.

"Hi, Miss Rectrix," said a deferential voice inside the room. "Just a reminder that dinner will be served at seven in the main dining room."

"Thanks," said Verna, sounding morose now.

"You know what this means, Dooley?" I said excitedly.

"No, what?" asked Dooley.

"We found the killer!"

"We did?"

"Sure!"

"So who is it?"

"Verna! She just said it: 'I did what you asked me to!' She killed Kimberlee because she thought her husband asked her to!"

"Or he could have told her to buy a Snickers bar and she got him a Milky Way instead."

"Oh, Dooley," I said with a laugh. Not such a great detective after all!

"What? It's true. Some people like Snickers, others like Milky Way."

"Let's jump to the next balcony and tell Odelia the good news. I'll bet she'll be so happy she'll jump to the roof."

"Why would Odelia jump on the roof?"

"It's just a figure of speech. Come on."

Verna's husband watched us hop up onto the balustrade, then to the next balcony. "Cats," he muttered again, then shook his head and soon was lost in what looked like very gloomy thoughts indeed. Like the fact that he'd ordered his wife to murder her girlfriend and she'd actually gone and done it!

The next balcony did not belong to Odelia either. It was another guest bedroom, and was occupied by a woman I immediately recognized as Alina Isman, the famous and extraordinary actress. She was quarreling with her husband. Today really seemed to be Fight-With-A-Spouse-Day. And since we were there anyway, we decided to stick around for a moment, and hear what they had to say to each other. We might learn something.

"I wonder where Harriet and Brutus are," said Dooley as we settled in for another close listen. "Aren't they supposed to be investigating, too?"

"I'll bet they're in the kitchen," I said, "looking for something to eat."

We shared a look and it soon became clear what our next port of call would be—after we'd delivered the good news to Odelia we'd identified the killer.

"I'm so, so sorry," said Alina's husband. "Can you ever forgive me?"

"I don't know if I can," she said coldly.

She was standing at the window looking out, her back straight, a pensive look in her eyes as she gazed out into the distance.

"I swear to God, I never laid a finger on that woman—not a finger!"

"Oh, spare me the crap, Reinhart," she said, turning on her heel and laying into him. "You laid more than a finger on her. In fact you laid all of your fingers on her, didn't you, all eleven of them!"

Dooley, next to me, was frowning. "Eleven fingers? I thought humans only had ten fingers?"

I didn't have the heart to explain about this elusive eleventh finger. I still had the whole birds and bees thing coming up, and didn't want to add this finger business to the list, so instead I said, "She probably sucks at math."

"No, that never happened," Reinhart protested. "Look, I admit I wanted to—and when she came on to me I was sorely tempted. But I was strong—for you and for the kids—for our family!"

"Oh, aren't you the big hero."

"I never gave into temptation!"

"You're lying, I can tell."

"I'm not!"

"Your ears are twitching."

"They're not," he said with a little laugh.

"They are, too." There was a pause. "So you and Kimberlee never…"

"Never," he said, and sounded earnest. "Besides, she was already having an affair with Verna at the time, and I didn't want to be just another notch on her belt, you know."

"So you wanted to have an affair but you decided she didn't like you enough, is that it?"

"That's not what I said. She tried to seduce me, and I told her in no uncertain terms no way, no how. I was married to one of her best friends, for crying out loud. She didn't seem to think that mattered one way or the other."

"She was never my friend," said Alina quietly. "I thought she was for a while, but now I see she was just playing me, like she played everyone she came into contact with. We were all simply means to an end. Stepping stones for her to reach the top. The only reason she wanted to sleep with you is because you're a very important recording artist, Reinhart. And you could have introduced her to a lot of very important people. Helped her career."

"Could being the keyword. I never gave into temptation, babe, I swear."

"Oh, Reinhart, you're such a jerk."

"I know, babe. But I'm your jerk."

"What am I going to do with you?"

I had the distinct impression the scene was about to turn

mushy so I told Dooley, "Let's go. There's nothing more for us to learn here."

Kissing sounds came from inside the room, and some moaning, too.

"I think Alina is in danger, Max," said Dooley. "We should do something."

"She'll be fine. This has got nothing to do with the case and everything to do with human frailty and the tendency to fall for the wrong person."

So we hopped the balustrade again and when we reached the next balcony I was over the moon to discover we'd finally reached our destination: inside Chase, Odelia and Gran were arguing about something.

"You have to tell them, Odelia!" Gran was saying. "It's not fair to keep them in the dark like this."

"I'll tell them when this is all over. When we're home."

"Better tell them now, or they'll never trust you again."

"Maybe I can tell them," said Chase, a smile in his voice.

They both ignored him. "Let's talk about this later," said Odelia.

"No, let's talk about this now. For the last time," said Gran, "you *have* to tell the cats the operation is irreversible. They'll *never* have baby cats. *Ever.*"

# CHAPTER 27

"Oh, hey, you guys," said Odelia when Max and Dooley stepped into the room. "Um... how much did you hear?"

"We heard everything," Max said ominously.

"They heard everything, right?" said Chase. "They don't look happy."

"You wouldn't look happy if you just overheard someone say you could never have babies," said Gran.

"Sorry," said Chase, a little lamely, then picked up Max and repeated, louder, "I'm very sorry about that, Max—but you can still lead a full and happy life, even though you can't have babies!"

"They're cats—not deaf," said Gran.

Chase put Max down again. "Sorry, buddy. This is all new for me."

"Look, just tell us already," said Max. "We're big cats. We can take it."

"I'm sorry," said Odelia, crouching down and sitting cross-legged. "The thing is, this operation you both had? It's irreversible."

"So the stuff Milo said…"

"No operation is going to fix this, no matter what Milo said."

"Harriet is not going to like this," said Max.

"Or Brutus," said Dooley.

Odelia eyed Dooley with concern. "Dooley, I know I should have had the talk with you a long time ago, but I always figured you were too young."

"Wait, you never had the talk with your cats?" asked Chase. "That's crazy!"

"Chase, shut up," said Gran.

"Shutting up," Chase muttered.

"What talk?" asked Dooley.

"This is the birds and bees thing I was telling you about," said Max.

"Look, when a man and a woman want to make a baby…" said Odelia.

"This is so weird," said Chase with a light chuckle.

"Chase," said Gran warningly.

"Or when a tomcat and a queen want to have a baby cat."

"Or half a million baby cats," said Max.

"So the thing is…" Odelia said. "Um…"

"Oh, just tell him already!" said Gran.

"Shut up, Gran."

"Maybe I'll tell them," Chase suggested. "Man to man, you know."

"Shut up, Chase," snapped Gran.

"The thing is…" said Odelia, then faltered again.

"It's not that hard," said Max. "Look, Dooley. You know how a bee flies from flower to flower right?"

"Uh-huh."

"And the bee takes a little bit of pollen from one flower and delivers it to another flower, and it sets in motion a process of creating new flowers?"

"Uh-huh," he said again, listening attentively.

"Well, the same thing happens when a male and a female of the species meet. The male takes the pollen to the female, and poof! A new baby is born."

"Ooh, I think I understand," said Dooley with a smile.

"Look at the little guy smiling," said Chase. "I didn't even know cats could smile, but look at him smiling."

"So what about Harriet? Does this mean Brutus can't bring her the pollen?"

Now it was Odelia's turn to get a little technical. "The thing is, just like flowers, females have a, um, receptacle for the, um, pollen. And the procedure removes the receptacle. It also removes the, um, pollen factory from the male."

Dooley nodded slowly. "So Brutus can't make new pollen, and Harriet can't receive it."

"That's right. That's exactly right," said Odelia, much relieved.

"Oh, man," said Dooley. "Looks like they're both screwed."

"Who is screwed?" asked a voice from the window. Two more cats came waltzing in. It was Harriet and Brutus.

"Uh-oh," said Dooley.

"Uh-oh," said Chase, who seemed to be on the same page as the cats and adjusting quickly to his newly acquired knowledge.

"It's actually very simple," said Dooley. "The operation removed your pollen receptacle, and it also removed Brutus's pollen factory. So now you can't have babies anymore, and no operation is going to fix that, no matter what Milo says. Isn't that right, Odelia?"

Harriet stared at Dooley for a moment, then cried, "WHAAAAAAT?!!!!!!"

"She's not taking it well," said Chase.

"No, she is not," said Gran. She glanced over to Chase. "Are you sure you don't understand what they're saying?"

"Positive. But it's not hard to interpret. They're so expressive!"

"Harriet, I'm very sorry, but it's true," said Odelia. "The operation was permanent. There are no tied-up tubes to untie, and the same goes for Brutus, and Max and Dooley, for that matter."

"But WHYYYYYYYY?!!!!!" Harriet wailed.

"Do you really want to fill the world with millions of cats who are never going to find a home because there simply aren't enough homes to go around?" asked Gran sternly. "Do you? Odelia did you a favor, young lady, and if you don't appreciate it, you better find yourself another home."

"Gran," said Odelia. "Let me handle this."

Harriet seemed on the verge of tears. But then she hardened. "Maybe I *will* look for a different home." And then she walked out onto the balcony again.

"Harriet!" cried Odelia, and hurried over. But when she got there, Harriet was gone. Like a ghost, she'd vanished into thin ear.

"Oh, damn," she said.

And when her grandmother and Chase joined her, Gran said, "Looks like someone threw a hissy fit."

"You should have let me handle it, Gran."

"You can't keep pussyfooting around it, Odelia. At some point you have to tell it like it is."

"I know, but there are different ways of handling a situation like this."

"She's gone," said Chase. "So weird." He looked up, then added, "Oh, there she is."

They all looked up, and true enough: Harriet was making her way up along the drainpipe.

"Harriet, get back here!" said Odelia.

"Fat chance, baby killer!" Harriet yelled, and hopped onto the roof.

"Don't worry," said Chase. "I'll get her."

And before Odelia could stop him, he was climbing that same drainpipe.

"Chase, get back here!" she yelled. "You're going to get yourself killed!"

"Just be a sec!" he said, then with surprising agility swung his leg over the gutter and disappeared from view.

"He's a hero," said Gran. "Or a moron. The jury is still out."

# CHAPTER 28

*H*arriet had reached the roof and was pondering her next course of action when Chase Kingsley, of all people, suddenly appeared and joined her.

"Nice view from up here," he said, wiping his hands and taking a seat.

"Yeah, pretty glorious," she said, wondering if he could suddenly understand her.

"The thing is, Harriet," he said, turning serious, "I can see where you're coming from. I'm in love with a pretty amazing person myself, and between you and me—and I hope you keep this to yourself—I hope one day to settle down with her and have lots of babies. So I understand your frustration, I really do. But you have to believe me when I tell you that Odelia doesn't have a malicious bone in her body. Not a one. She's the most loving, caring and sweet-natured person I know. Pure goodness through and through. She would never have done this if she didn't believe in her heart it was the right thing to do."

"She took away my happiness," said Harriet sadly. "My one chance at happiness."

"I hear you, babe," said Chase, "but look at it from her side: she wanted to spare you a life of unhappiness. Being pregnant all the time, wearing yourself out, being followed around by all the horny bastards of the neighborhood."

She laughed at this. "You're funny."

"And trust me, there's a lot of horny bastards out here—a lot."

"There's only one horny bastard I care about and that's Brutus," she said. "But keep this to yourself, will you? I don't want him to get too cocky."

"And I hope you'll forgive me for sounding cocky, but I think I'm something of an expert on all things Odelia and if she says this is what's best for you, she's probably right. So please please please don't go looking for another home. It will break Odelia's heart. She loves you guys to death, and would do anything for you. You know that, right?"

"Yeah, I guess I do," said Harriet. "It's just that, I had this dream, you know, and now it's pretty much shattered, and now I don't know what to do."

"We could always adopt," he said. "I don't know how it works for cats, but we could adopt a kitten and she could come and live with us. You and Brutus could raise her and that way you'd have your own family, just like you want."

"I guess I'd be okay with that," she admitted. To be totally honest, she wasn't really looking forward to being pregnant and delivering half a dozen babies. She'd seen friends of hers that hadn't been spayed get pregnant and the novelty quickly wore off, as did the joy of having offspring in the double digits. At first it was all great fun, but then it just became a drag. And Chase was right. It wore you down, being pregnant all the time. So maybe he had a point. Maybe Odelia had done the right thing, or what she thought was right.

"So what do you say, princess?" he said, holding out a hand. "Do you want to reconsider and rejoin your family?

Cause make no mistake, Odelia and Gran and Marge and Tex and me—we are your family."

"And Max and Dooley and Brutus," she added softly.

"Yeah, them, too."

"You're making progress, you goofy cop," said Harriet, putting her paw in Chase's big mitt.

"Let's get you down, shall we?"

"No way," she said with a laugh. "Let's make them sweat for a while. Something you need to learn, buddy. You can't give in too soon. Or else they'll think you're a pushover."

He eyed her curiously. "You're a lot smarter than they give you credit for."

"And you're pretty smart for a non-cat-talking cop," she said.

It seemed they had reached an understanding, and when ten minutes later, huffing and puffing, Odelia's head cleared the roof, and she asked, "What the hell are you two doing up here? Organizing a lemonade stand?"

"Just chatting," said Harriet.

"He doesn't even speak your language!" Odelia cried, panting heavily.

"He doesn't have to. We had a heart to heart—no language required."

"We had a great chat," said Chase. "I have no idea what she said, but somehow I know exactly what she said, if you know what I mean."

Odelia rolled onto the roof and onto her back. "I know exactly what you mean, both of you. And now can we please get down? Dinner is served and I'm starving!"

"Dinner!" Harriet cried, and instantly got up and walked over to Odelia. "Why didn't you tell me sooner?"

"Dinner?" asked Chase.

"Dinner," said Odelia. "The magic word."

"Figures," said Chase.

Cats or humans. They were a lot more alike than most people thought.

# CHAPTER 29

"So where were you guys?" I asked once Harriet had decided to come down off her high horse—or, in her case, the roof.

"Oh, here and there," said Brutus vaguely.

Odelia, Chase and Gran were getting ready for dinner, and so were us cats. Only we had a lot less work preparing ourselves then they had, obviously.

"We discovered the truth about the murder," said Dooley proudly.

"No way. You mean you know who did it?" asked Brutus.

"Yes, we do," I said.

"So who was it?" asked Brutus.

"Verna Rectrix. We heard it from her own lips."

"Oh, wow," he said. Then, after a pause, "Who is Verna Rectrix?"

"She's this amazing actress who plays one of the main characters in *Big Little Secrets*," said Harriet. "I love her. She's quirky, does yoga, and is a vegetarian—or a vegan? She has spunk and pizzazz—are you sure she did it?"

"Yeah, she said it herself. Apparently her husband told her

to—or so she thought. So she killed Kimberlee and now it turns out it was all a big misunderstanding."

"What a horrible story," said Harriet.

"So what else did you and Chase talk about on the roof?" Brutus asked.

"This and that," she said.

"Oh, come on," said Brutus. "Don't be like that, Harriet. We don't have secrets from each other, do we?"

"We don't have secrets from each other either, Brutus," I reminded him.

He gave me a guilty look. "Okay, if you have to know, we visited Emerald's room."

"So while we were investigating a murder you two were sightseeing?" I should have known. Harriet always does whatever she likes.

"I just wanted to see how she lives," said Harriet. "She's such an amazing actress and I've always been such a fan. This is, like, a once-in-a-lifetime opportunity to check out this true legend's private space, you guys."

"And? How was it?"

"Very nice," said Brutus.

"Yeah, she lives well," Harriet chimed in. "Her room is probably three times as big as this one. It's on the other side of the staircase. She has her own private bathroom, which is just amazing—and huge."

"There's also a gigantic bedroom with an amazingly soft bed."

"And an entire room just to fit all of her clothes. You should see the size of it—there's easily thousands of dresses in there, and the most gorgeous outfits. And shoes. Oh, my God so many shoes!"

"There's also a private dining room with a window that overlooks the pool and gardens. I mean, this is something else, you guys."

"We saw her personal stash of Coke Emerald. There's a roomful of them, and she keeps them chilled, the AC at full blast. That woman loves Coke."

"There was a maid there, which is how we got in. But then she saw us and started chasing us around with a broom! So we had to hide out on the balcony, which is how we got back here—hopping from balcony to balcony."

I stared at Brutus for a moment. "Do you think that's how Verna got into Kimberlee's room? By climbing over the balcony? That would explain how the door was locked from the inside."

"I'm sure Uncle Alec looked into that," said Harriet.

"Yeah, I guess he would," I said. But I was still going to mention it to Odelia when I got the chance. With this whole Harriet drama I hadn't found the right opportunity to talk to Odelia about our big discovery either.

"I wonder if Coke Emerald tastes different from regular Coke," said Dooley, harping on a topic I thought we'd exhausted already.

"It's a little sweeter," said Harriet.

"And how would you know?" I asked.

"Cause I tasted it, of course!" said Harriet. "Emerald poured some into a bowl for her doggie. So I had a lick and it tastes exactly like Coke but sweeter."

"Yeah, sweeter," Brutus confirmed.

"You drank from a dog bowl?" asked Dooley, shocked.

"It's a clean dog," said Harriet defensively. "I'll bet Emerald's dog is probably the most pampered, cleanest dog in the country, maybe the world."

"The whole apartment was clean," said Brutus. "Squeaky clean."

"You could eat off the floor," Harriet added. "Not that I did, though."

"So is everything settled now?" I asked. "About the baby situation?"

"We're going to adopt," said Harriet, entwining her tail with Brutus's. "Isn't that right, sweetums?"

"Chase's idea. And I like it," said Brutus. "That way we'll have our own little family and we won't have to give away dozens of kittens to the pound."

"Lady cats never have a dozen kittens, silly," said Harriet.

"They don't? I thought that was about the size of a single litter."

"More like three, four, five... sometimes more."

Brutus gulped, clearly happy he'd dodged a bullet. Fathering half a dozen kittens takes a lot out of a gentleman cat, and Brutus wasn't exactly the father type. Then again, maybe he was. We'd soon find out.

"I can't wait to select a kitten," said Dooley now.

"It's our kitten, Dooley," said Harriet. "Not yours or Max's or even Odelia's. Ours. So we'll be the ones to pick it out. Isn't that right, angel bunny?"

"Exactly right, buttercup," said Brutus, and I had the impression he was already dreading the moment he came face to face with his future offspring.

$\mathcal{A}$s we headed down the stairs to go into dinner, we attracted a lot of attention. It probably wasn't a common practice for one of Emerald's guests to come loaded with furry felines as opposed to fluffy canines. Whereas Verna, Abbey, Alina and Emerald all carried their respective furballs in their arms, Harriet, Dooley, Brutus and myself walked down the stairs under our own steam—which just goes to show, once more, that cats really are the superior species when compared to the canine of the animal kingdom.

"Oh, by the way, Odelia," I said as we traipsed down. "Dooley and I have solved the case."

"You have?" said Odelia, sounding surprised. "That was quick."

"Yeah, we just happened to be there when Verna Rectrix admitted guilt." And in a few brief words I told her what we'd overheard Verna and her husband Thaw Roman discuss. I also mentioned our little chat with Kimberlee's dog Stevie about the person who was in the room with her when she died and how they talked about Kimberlee directing something.

"Well, I'll be damned," said Odelia. "Sounds like you're right. Verna did it."

"Which still doesn't explain how she did it," said Gran. "I mean, that locked door is still a mystery to me."

"We'll figure it out. But this is an important break-through. Well done, you guys."

"Or is it? Verna could have been referring to something else entirely."

I decided to write off Gran's skepticism as sour grapes because she hadn't been the one to crack the case. As usual, it was us, the cats, who'd found the telling clue. But then wasn't that usually the case?

"What are you guys talking about?" asked Chase.

"Max and Dooley have cracked the case," said Odelia.

Chase lifted an eyebrow. "You don't say."

"I do say." She paused for suspense. "It was Verna."

"Verna Rectrix?"

"Yup."

And while Odelia gave her boyfriend an update, we'd arrived downstairs and humans and animals were separated at the entrance to the dining room: cats and dogs to the left, humans to the right. So we waved goodbye to Odelia, Gran and Chase, and followed one of Emerald's people into an area of the kitchen that appeared to have been reserved specifically for Emerald's pets, and those visiting pets who were lucky enough to be invited along with their masters.

"Oh, my God," Harriet exclaimed when we entered what could only be described as pet heaven. Beautiful bowls were lined up along the wall, and a whole team of servers stood at attention, ready to cater to our every need.

"We have consulted with your owners as to your dietary needs and particular desires," said the person in charge of this bucolic feast, a heavily mustachioed individual dressed in pristine white. "And we have selected those precious morsels we humbly hope will appeal to your delicate palates. I've also taken the liberty of consulting with leading nutritionists and pet food designers, and have prepared a meal that I think will be to your liking." He cracked a tight smile and took a stiff-backed bow. "Bon appétit."

There was indeed a bowl with my name on it, and when I walked over I discovered to my not inconsiderable surprise that it contained the yummiest, juiciest, most exquisite-looking, delicious-tasting, heavenly-smelling nuggets of food I'd ever seen, tasted or smelled in my entire life. Soon the only sounds that could be heard were the sounds of four cats and five dogs digging into their respective bowls and eating to their heart's content. I would have complimented the chef, if I hadn't been too busy devouring what was without a doubt the best meal of my life. And when finally I'd reached the bottom of my bowl, one of those wonderful servers stood at attention to inquire if I wanted more, and if so, how much.

"More," I said between two bites. "Just keep it coming, please."

The server, clearly instructed not to stint on the good stuff, complied.

I was determined to keep eating until there was nothing left. An ambitious proposition, no doubt, but one I vowed to see through to the end.

And judging from the concerted effort and absolute focus of my pet-mates, they had the exact same thing in mind.

"Oh, boy," said Dooley as he looked up, his nose covered in yummy food, "I think we picked the wrong humans to live with, Max."

"I'm starting to think so, too," I said, then busied myself with devouring this second helping, which tasted slightly different than the first, only because the server had managed to surprise me once again.

"And this is only the entree," she said as she watched me

eat with a gratified smile. "There's more to come. Lots and lots and lots more. Emerald believes in spoiling her pets rotten, you see, so this is just the beginning."

"I love Emerald," I said huskily. "My god how I love this woman. She is the queen, the top, the absolute pinnacle of pet care."

And then I dug in once more. Who has time to stand around flapping their gums when they can use those same gums for eating!

&.

*I*n the main dining room conversations were a little stilted. After everything that had happened these ladies, Hollywood royalty as Emerald referred to them, were visibly shook by the death of one of their own, even if they hadn't liked her all that much.

Odelia was seated next to Emerald and even the queen of the silver screen was unusually quiet.

"I thought about canceling the weekend," she admitted as she dug into her Cajun shrimp and rice. "But that just wouldn't be fair to the rest of us. It's not because one selfish person decided to ruin it for us—more specifically me—that I should give in and admit defeat. Kimberlee wanted to destroy me, and I'll be damned if I'm going to let her."

"You still think she did it on purpose?" asked Odelia, not wanting to reveal Kimberlee's death had actually been a murder—a murder she'd since solved.

"I'm starting to think so more and more. Like Alina said this afternoon, why single out this weekend and my home to commit this act of cowardice? Obviously she wanted to end her life a long time ago, but to choose this specific time and place... That is simply rude. Very bad manners indeed."

It was the first time Odelia had ever heard someone refer

to suicide as bad manners and to the victim as being rude, but she refrained from comment.

To her right, Gran was tucking in with relish. All this talk of death had clearly not put her off her appetite.

"Now this is what I call some great chow," she muttered.

"Yeah, the food is pretty amazing," Chase agreed. "In fact I can't think of a time I've had better meals—beats the best restaurants in town."

"So are you also in the movie business?" asked Verna's husband, leaning over to direct the question at Gran, who clearly had everyone puzzled with her suddenly turning up.

"Oh, God, no," said Gran with a laugh. "As if. Though I'm thinking about launching a career. Seeing all these gorgeous women light up the screen, I'm inspired."

Thaw appeared confused.

"So if you're not an actress…"

"I'm Odelia's grandmother. She needed my help, so here I am."

"How fascinating," the actor said.

"So, Emerald," said Gran now, wiping her lips with her napkin.

"Mh?" said the screen goddess, looking up from her musings on Kimberlee's ultimate betrayal.

"Any pointers for a newbie? I'm thinking about launching myself in the biz," she clarified.

"Pointers? Oh, you mean acting tips." She thought for a moment. "Always be yourself and don't take crap from anyone. Especially directors, producers or studio heads. She directed a pointed look at Odo Hardy, her director, who was seated to her right. He graciously kept his tongue at this harangue.

"Yeah, that shouldn't be a problem for me," said Gran. "I never take crap from anyone, and I'm always true to myself. Rules to live by, right?"

She then ogled the director for a moment. "Say, listen. Do you have a part for me in your next movie, director dude?"

Odo looked up. "Well, currently I'm working on a remake of *Cleopatra*. And even though a lot of the roles have been cast, we're still looking for someone to play the role of Cleopatra's mother. I've been trying to entice Helen Mirren to sign up for the part, but so far she's proving reluctant."

"So who's playing Cleopatra?"

"We've cast Alicia Vikander for the role," he said. "I think she'll be great."

Emerald pulled a sour face. "If I were a few years younger, I could have played her."

"I don't understand why you have to pick a white actress," said Verna peevishly. "Cleopatra was Egyptian, right? Why not pick an actress of color?"

"You mean like yourself?" said Emerald. "As if you are good enough to play such a plummy part."

Verna stiffened visibly, threw down her utensils and got up. "You know what? I think I've had enough of your abuse, Emerald. Come on, Thaw. Let's get out of here."

"But you can't go!" said Emerald, clearly sorry about her outburst.

"That wasn't a very nice thing to say, Emerald," said Abbey.

"No, not very nice at all," Alina added.

"I apologize! I'm sorry, Verna," said Emerald. "It's just that I have so much on my plate right now. I didn't mean what I said, darling. You know I love you."

Verna hesitated for a moment, then returned to her seat.

"You really should cast a woman of color as Cleopatra," she repeated. "In this day and age, whitewashing will only get you pilloried by your audience."

"I could play Cleopatra," said Gran. "I think I'd be great."

"I don't..." The director looked at her with a bemused

expression on his face. "Wouldn't you say you're a little ... old for the part, Mrs. Muffin?"

"That's ageism right there," said Gran. "I think it's time Hollywood starts to appreciate senior citizens. We're a large chunk of audience that goes absolutely unserved. Casting me as Cleopatra would give a signal. A signal that senior citizens count in Hollywood. That we haven't been forgotten."

"You should cast a senior citizen woman of color," said Verna. "That way you'd hit the two demographics in one fell swoop."

Odelia glanced over to Verna, and thought back to Max's words. They sounded pretty damning. But before she talked to Uncle Alec, she needed to be absolutely sure. She needed to hear it from the woman's lips. So she vowed to have a little chat with Verna later on and ask her straight out. She was pretty sure she'd be able to tell if she was lying or not.

Then again, Verna was a professional actress.

To convincingly tell a lie came with the territory.

# CHAPTER 31

*T*hat night, Emerald had planned a movie night in her private movie theater. It should have been a fun night for all, but now of course no one was in the mood. Instead, one after the other people drifted off to bed. Tomorrow was the last day, and even though the itinerary said there was horse riding planned, and a trip to the nearby town of Happy Bays, Odelia had the distinct impression there wouldn't be much horse riding or visits to quaint little towns.

Verna and her husband had been sitting huddled together on the terrace, nursing their drinks and talking intensely, and the moment Thaw got up, Odelia saw her opportunity and seized it by approaching the actress.

"I'm so sorry," she said by way of introduction, "but I couldn't help overhearing you and your husband arguing this afternoon."

Verna frowned. "You did?"

"I was in my room, on the balcony, and I couldn't help but hear you say to Thaw that you did what he asked you to." She lifted a meaningful eyebrow.

"So?"

"So I should probably tell you that I don't think Kimberlee's death was a suicide. I actually think she was murdered…"

Verna's face cleared as understanding dawned. Astonishment mingled with amusement on the actress's face. "You think I killed Kimberlee? Seriously?"

Odelia shrugged. "Before I talk to my uncle I wanted to talk to you first. I know how words can get twisted and lost in translation, so…"

"You came to elicit a confession from me," said Verna, nodding. She glanced down to Odelia's chest. "Are you wearing a wire? Is this a sting?"

"Of course not. I just wanted to give you the opportunity to explain before I talked to the police about what I heard."

Verna leaned back and tucked her legs underneath her. "And a good thing you did, or else you would have made an absolute fool of yourself, Miss Poole. What Thaw and I were discussing was actually our divorce."

"Your divorce?"

"The thing is… I had a brief affair with Kimberlee."

"I know. I mean, so I've been told."

"My, my. Aren't you the busy bee?"

"There's been a lot of talk this weekend."

Verna leveled a critical look at her fellow actresses. "Oh, how they love to talk." She hesitated for a moment, then said, "When Thaw found out about the affair, he went ahead and hired a lawyer. When he told me, I…" She shook her head. "It was as if I woke up from a trance. I realized I loved Thaw, and that this thing I had with Kimberlee was just a fling. So I promised Thaw I'd break it off and do whatever it took to make it up to him. I went into therapy and—"

"Wait, *you* broke it off?"

"I did, yes."

"But I thought…"

"I know what you thought—what everybody thinks. That Kimberlee dumped me. But that's not what happened. I was the one to end it—because I didn't want to lose Thaw. And then Kimberlee started spreading vicious lies about me behind my back. Saying things like how I'd been unfaithful. How I was an addict—trying to sabotage my career, you know. Out of spite."

"So that's why you blew up at her. Not because she dumped you but—"

"Because she was trying to make me out to be someone I'm not. And I wanted her to stop."

"So when you said to your husband 'I did what you asked me to…'"

"I was referring to me breaking up with Kimberlee and starting therapy. Not," she added emphatically, "murdering Kimberlee—I mean, really?"

"I'm sorry. It just sounded as if…"

Verna studied Odelia with an amused expression on her face. "You have quite the imagination, Miss Poole, but then I guess for a reporter that comes with the territory."

"Odelia, please, and I'm sorry if I offended you. I just thought…"

Verna waved her apologies away. "It's fine. At least you didn't slap a pair of handcuffs on my wrists. But tell me— why would you think Kimberlee was murdered? I thought it was pretty obvious she killed herself."

"A hunch, mainly," said Odelia. She didn't want to mention that Kimberlee's dog had heard her mistress talk to a mystery visitor immediately before she died. It was not the kind of revelation that would stand up in court.

"Yeah, I guess reporters develop good hunches. Does your uncle think the same thing?"

"Yes, he does."

"So it's official?"

"Well… Officially nothing has been decided yet."

"Murder." She shook her head, her dreadlocks dangling pleasantly. "Incredible. But who would do that to her?"

"Take your pick," said Odelia, gesturing at the people still present on the terrace. "From what I can tell Kimberlee wasn't exactly Miss Popular."

"She wasn't. I had all the reason in the world to hate her, and so did a lot of other people."

"So what do you think? Assuming it was murder. Who is the killer?"

Verna thought for a moment. "If I had to hazard a guess, I'd say her boyfriend. The poor guy has had to endure so much over the years. She made a complete fool of him over and over and over again."

They both studied Kimberlee's boyfriend Zoltan, who was sitting by himself, sipping from a vodka tonic and looking every inch the tragic widower.

"He just doesn't seem like the type, though," said Verna.

"They never do," said Odelia, speaking from experience.

# CHAPTER 32

*I* have to admit that in spite of the fact that we were now the guests of an obviously very accomplished hostess, I still missed my own homestead that night. There simply isn't anything better than to take a nice snooze on your favorite spot on the couch or the foot of the bed. And I know that the beds and the couches in this part of the world were of a much better quality than those belonging to my own human, but what can I say? Sometimes that ratty old jacket you've been wearing for years is preferable to that brand-new and very expensive coat.

I'm obviously not speaking from experience here. Cats don't wear jackets or coats. But you catch my drift.

Still, I'd found a nice little spot on Odelia's very large and very comfy bed, Dooley had taken up position at Chase's feet, and Harriet and Brutus had decided to make full use of the large space on Gran's bed next door.

We'd all had such a nice and filling dinner we were satisfied to sleep it off for a couple of hours, this murder business the furthest thing from our minds.

Odelia and Chase talked deep into the night, but I didn't

let it keep me from enjoying a refreshing slumber. So when I did finally awake, I found that both my humans had drifted off to sleep, and only one pair of eyes was staring at me in wonder. I had no problem attributing the inquisitive peepers to my friend Dooley, who obviously had been awake for quite a little while.

"What's wrong, Dooley?" I asked, yawning and stretching. "Why are you up?"

"You are the soundest sleeper I know, Max," he said reverently.

"I know," I said. "I like sleeping."

"You really sleep the sleep of the dead."

"I'm not sure I like that particular simile."

"For a moment there? I thought you were really dead. You weren't dead, were you, though, Max?"

"If I was dead I'd still be dead right now. Being dead is not a temporary affliction, Dooley. In most cases it's permanent."

"People have come back from the dead," he argued.

"Yeah, but they usually had to be brought back by an able team of medical professionals and quite a few shocks to the system. Spontaneously dying and then equally spontaneously reviving would be akin to a medical miracle."

"I'm glad you're not dead, Max."

"That makes two of us. So what's up? Can't sleep?"

"I thought I heard a noise."

I turned my antenna-like ears in the direction he was indicating. He was right. There was a noise, and it seemed to be coming from the wall dividing this room from the next, where Gran was presumably sleeping soundly.

"Could be Gran snoring," I said.

"Or Brutus."

"Does Brutus snore?"

"He does." He giggled. "The funniest little snuffles."

We both jumped down from the bed and padded over to

the wall. I put one ear against it and listened intently.

"It doesn't sound like snoring," I finally determined. "More like... munching."

"Maybe Gran grinding her teeth?"

"Could be if she had teeth."

"She doesn't?"

"She does, but she puts them in a cup every night."

"That would probably prevent her from grinding them."

"It would."

"Could be mice," I finally determined. Chewing in the middle of the night? Either mice or rats. Now I was totally intrigued. So I hunkered down and saw there was a crack underneath the baseboard. And since cats will be cats, I inserted a nail and started pulling. That's what we like to do: we like to dig our nails in and tug and see what happens.

"I'll bet it's mice," I said.

"Or a secret door to a secret room."

Doubtful, but I could tell Dooley was more excited about the prospect of a secret room than a family of mice so I said, "Now wouldn't that be cool?"

"The coolest!" Dooley said, and followed my lead.

The secret door, if that was what it was, didn't budge, though. It probably was locked and needed a key or some secret ritual to open it all the way. And if it was mice, as I suspected, they'd found the perfect hiding place: one where even cats couldn't reach.

"What's going on, you guys?" asked a sleepy voice from the bed.

"Oh, just that we've discovered a secret door," Dooley said casually.

This made Odelia sit up right away and flick on the bedside lamp.

"What's happening?" muttered a sleepy Chase. "Why are we getting up?"

"The cats have discovered a secret door."

"Secret door? What is this? A Nancy Drew story?"

Odelia had padded over barefoot and now crouched down next to us. She rubbed her finger along the crack. "Looks like you're right. But how to open it?"

"We've been trying," said Dooley, "but they must have locked it really tight."

"Has to be a way to open it somehow," said Odelia, her fingers gently exploring the surface of the alleged secret door.

Chase, who'd reluctantly thrown off the blanket of sleep and also his actual blanket, joined us. "Lemme see," he said. He studied the wall for a moment, then poked his finger at a part of the wallpaper depicting a flower bud. There was a click and a whirr, and suddenly the door swung open!

"Well, I'll be damned," said Odelia, appropriately impressed.

"Magic finger," Chase announced proudly.

Odelia opened the door further and we found ourselves staring into a darkened space. We all popped our heads in to take a look-see. In the dark, I could see a small hairy form run for cover. It was a mouse. Our mysterious muncher. I decided not to tell the others. At heart, I'm a peace-loving cat.

"A secret corridor," said Chase. "This *is* a Nancy Drew story."

"Or a Hardy Boys story," Odelia allowed.

Whatever it was, we'd made the most astonishing discovery.

"You know what this means, right?" I said.

They all looked at me. Even Chase, who seemed to have developed a sudden fascination for our thoughts and suggestions.

"This must be how the killer got into Kimberlee's room!"

# CHAPTER 33

"You know what? I think you're right, Max," said Odelia.

"Of course I'm right," said Max.

"Is he saying this is how the killer got into Kimberlee's room?" asked Chase.

"How did you—can you suddenly understand my cats?" asked Odelia, stunned.

"No, but it seems like the logical conclusion for the locked room mystery. This is the only way the killer—if there was a killer—could have snuck into the room."

"Well, there was a killer," she pointed out. "Kimberlee's dog said so."

Chase laughed. "I'm sorry. I still have to get used to this whole 'Max said this' and 'the dog said that' thing. As if I've just entered a Dr. Dolittle movie. And you don't even look like Eddie Murphy."

"We need to follow this lead," said Odelia. "Find out how far this goes."

"I'll bet these corridors run all over the house," said Chase.

"We better call Uncle Alec," said Odelia. "He needs to search these corridors for clues."

"I'll bet the killer, whoever he or she is, was careful enough not to leave any clues," said Chase. He'd picked up his phone, launched the flashlight app, and shone it down the corridor. It looked exactly like what it was: a space between two walls, high enough and wide enough for a single person to pass through.

"I wonder why Emerald had these constructed," said Odelia.

"Emerald didn't build this house," said Chase. "She bought it a little under a decade ago. This house is easily a hundred years old. Emerald and Pete, when they got it, did a lot of renovations, though, but I'll bet these corridors were never touched."

"How do you know so much about this?"

"Because I talked to Steve and he told me."

"Maybe the original owner was some old pervert who liked to spy on his guests?" Max suggested.

Odelia laughed. Chase did not. She repeated Max's words and he grinned. "I'm starting to understand why you like those cats so much. They're hilarious."

"And very clever," she said as she closed the secret door again and it locked into place. "They found this passageway, didn't they?"

"So this is how you managed to solve all of those mysteries. You had help from your 'secret sources.'"

Now it was her turn to grin. "I couldn't very well tell you that my secret sources were my cats, could I? Besides, you would never have believed me."

"It's ingenious," he admitted. "Cats are able to go anywhere undetected, and the bad guys won't think twice to discuss their nefarious plans in front of a cat or household pet, knowing they won't spread the word."

"Only they do spread the word, and very happily so."

Just then, Odelia thought she saw movement near the door. When she walked over, and opened it, she didn't see anything. What she did detect were voices, whispering in the dark. She listened intently. And then she heard it.

"Don't worry about a thing, my darling. I was very careful not to leave a single trace."

"I worry about you, that's all."

"Like I said, nothing to worry about. They'll never know."

"I hope you're right."

Odelia quickly darted into the hallway and peered into the darkness. She heard a door close, but it was impossible to know which one it was.

"What's going on?" asked Chase, following her out.

"I heard two people talking," she said. "But now they're gone."

"What did they say?"

"The woman said something about how she'd been very careful and how they'd never catch her. The guy seemed worried and she was reassuring him."

He gave her a thoughtful look. "Do you think it was the killer?"

"Could be," she said. "Whoever it was, they're gone now, and..."

They'd returned to the room and suddenly she saw a white envelope on the floor. Someone must have slipped it under the door. So that was the movement she'd seen. With a frown, she picked it up. It was addressed 'To Miss Poole, Reporter.'

"Well, open it," said Chase.

She did, and found a note inside. On it, the words were written: 'Please meet me at ten o'clock in the smoking room. It's important. Shauna.'

"Who's Shauna?" asked Chase.

"I have no idea," said Odelia as she turned the small piece of paper over in her hands. She thought for a moment. "Maybe one of the maids?"

"Do you think she's the one you heard talking just now?"

"I'm not sure. I don't think so. She probably came up, put this note under the door and disappeared again as fast as she could."

"Tomorrow we'll know more," said Chase. "And now we better get some sleep."

He was right. She felt frustrated, though, and had half a mind to go in search of this Shauna person right now, and ask her what she knew or thought she knew. Then again, she had no idea where to find her, and didn't feel like waking up Emerald. For all she knew Emerald was the killer. At this point they couldn't rule out anyone. Except maybe Verna.

The door next to their room opened, and Gran poked her head out. "What's with all the whispering?" she complained. "A person can't even get a good night's sleep in this place for all the whispering."

"I'm sorry, Gran," said Odelia. "There's been a development."

Gran, who was dressed in funky fluorescent PJs, her tiny white curls covered with a hairnet, held out her hand as Odelia handed her the little note.

"Looks like your killer was seen by this Shauna person," said Gran. "Which begs the question: why didn't she tell the cops?"

"Maybe she doesn't trust cops?" said Chase. "Some people don't."

"We also found a corridor that presumably connects all rooms," said Odelia.

"So that's how the killer did it," said Gran. "I knew there had to be a logical explanation for that darned locked door."

It appeared there was nothing more they could do, so

they returned to their respective rooms and back to bed. It took a while for Odelia to find sleep again. And as she finally drifted off, she dreamed of secret corridors and secret rooms and silent killers who moved through the house like the wind.

# CHAPTER 34

*T*he next morning, Odelia was awakened when a hand shook her. She reluctantly opened her eyes and muttered, "Need. More. Sleep."

When she saw Chase's serious expression, all thought of sleep was immediately wiped from her mind. She sat up with a jerk. "What's wrong?"

She saw Uncle Alec had also entered the room. He looked equally grave.

"There's been an accident," said Chase.

He gave her a look of significance and she instantly clapped a hand to her mouth. "Not..."

He nodded. "Shauna Shostak. You were right. She was one of the maids. She was found early this morning at the foot of the basement stairs, her neck broken."

"Was she..."

"She could have fallen down the stairs," said Uncle Alec, "or she could have been pushed. Too soon to tell."

"We did find a brick next to her head with blood on it, and she has a nasty wound on the side of the head," said Chase.

"So she could have been shoved down the stairs than finished off by smashing her head in with the brick," said Odelia.

Uncle Alec nodded. "Which was unnecessary. Cause of death is a broken neck. Could be that she hit her head on the way down, of course. Like I said, it's too soon to tell."

Odelia had gotten up and quickly got dressed in jeans and a T-shirt. A glance at her phone told her it was early. Seven o'clock.

"Who found her?"

"A cook," said Uncle Alec. "Just after six. She called it in and I called Chase."

The cats, seated at the foot of the bed, intently listening, were wide awake.

"What can we do?" asked Max seriously.

"Yeah, how can we help?" asked Dooley.

She thought for a moment. "Keep doing what you did yesterday. Put your ear to the ground. Listen to the chatter." To Chase and her uncle, she added, "If Shauna saw something, maybe she told others—or maybe one of her colleagues saw the same thing and hasn't come forward yet."

"We're interviewing all of them," said Uncle Alec.

"So you're not treating this as a suicide anymore?"

Uncle Alec hesitated. "The thing is, so far all we have to go on is the word of Kimberlee's dog. Not enough to open an official investigation, I'm afraid."

"So we'll keep on digging," said Odelia determinedly. "Shauna gave her life trying to tell me what she knew. We owe it to her to stop this killer."

"So you think Shauna was killed by the same person who killed Kimberlee?" asked Uncle Alec.

"I do. Shauna must have seen something or heard something and was going to reveal it to me. The killer must have found out and couldn't let her go through with it. Doing the right thing cost the poor woman her life."

"Why don't we let Odelia talk to some of Shauna's colleagues?" Chase suggested. "They might open up to her. Like I told your mom last night, some people don't like talking to cops."

"Good idea," said Alec.

Together, they made their way down the stairs. On the way, they met a distraught-looking Abbey. "So it's true? Someone else died?"

"It's true," Odelia confirmed.

"This place is quickly turning into the castle of doom!" said Abbey, though she had the excited air of a person eager to be in the thick of things. She joined Odelia as she descended the stairs. "So what happened?"

"One of the maids fell down the stairs and broke her neck."

"A maid?" Abbey seemed mildly disappointed. When Odelia nodded affirmatively, she said, "You know what? I think I left something in my room."

She'd clearly hoped for a more juicy story than a maid falling down the stairs. Odelia watched her leave with mixed feelings. Even though she kinda liked Abbey, she was one of her suspects. Shaking her head, she quickly hurried to catch up with her uncle and Chase.

She followed them into the kitchen, and then to the smoker's room where Shauna had asked her to meet. Seated there, smoking and looking distraught, was a woman with a white cook's uniform, her eyes red and puffy.

"This is Sylvia," said Uncle Alec. "She's the one who found Shauna. And this is Odelia," he introduced Odelia. "She's my niece and she'll ask you a couple of questions if that's okay with you."

The woman glanced up at Odelia. "Of course. Anything to help."

Odelia took a seat across the table from Sylvia and Chase and Alec left, closing the door behind them. The room smelled to cigarettes, and Odelia wondered why Emerald would keep a smoker's room in the house.

"Poor Shauna," said Sylvia. "She was just the sweetest little thing."

"You knew her well?"

"I did." She took a cigarette from a pack on the table. "Want one?"

"No, thanks," she said. "I don't smoke."

"Neither did Shauna. She spent an awful lot of time in here, though."

"Why was that?"

"I guess she liked to hang out with us. There's only three of us that smoke in the whole house, and when she was on her break Shauna always came down here and joined us. I once asked if she wasn't afraid of second-hand smoke but she didn't care. She was a sweet girl but she didn't get along with some of the others—especially Helen. She's the housekeeper. A real hellcat."

"I had no idea this place had a smoker's room," said Odelia.

"Emerald didn't like it, but if she wanted to keep Chef happy, she had to keep it. She wanted us to smoke outside, but Chef doesn't like freezing his rocks off just because he's a smoker. So he told Emerald either she organized a smoker's room or he was going to walk. She organized the room."

"So Shauna slipped this note under my door last night," said Odelia, deciding to tackle this thing head-on.

She placed the note in front of the cook, who read it eagerly. "Oh, that poor, stupid girl."

"Why do you say that?"

"She must have seen something, and instead of coming right out and telling the police she must have been chewing on it all day yesterday, only to finally decide to come forward in this roundabout way. And it got her killed."

"Did she tell you what it was that she saw, or heard?"

Sylvia bit her lip and shook her head. "If she'd told me I'd have advised her to go straight to the police."

"Why didn't she?"

The woman stubbed out her cigarette in an overflowing ashtray. "It's a big step to talk to the police—especially when you're a small cog in a big machine. My guess is she wasn't sure of what she saw, and didn't want to get in trouble with Helen or Emerald. So she decided to talk to you first."

"You don't think she fell, do you?"

Sylvia slowly shook her head. "No, I don't."

"This is very important," said Odelia, leaning forward. "Do you have any idea who might have done this to her?"

Sylvia stared at Odelia for a moment, then lit up another cigarette and directed a plume of smoke at the ceiling. "No, I don't, unfortunately."

"If you knew, you would tell me, right? I'm not a cop, Sylvia. Whatever you tell me stays between us. I promise you."

Sylvia flashed a quick smile. "I know. Shauna talked a lot about you. She was a big fan. Read all of your articles. And if I had any idea what happened I would happily tell you, but unfortunately I don't. All because Shauna didn't trust me enough to tell me what was going on." She hung her head. "And for that I'll always blame myself."

Odelia took the woman's hand. "Please don't. This is not your fault."

Sylvia looked up, and there were tears in her eyes. "If only she'd confided in me, I would have gone straight to the cops and she'd still be alive." They sat for a few moments in silence, then Sylvia said, in a throaty voice, "Please get whoever did this to my friend, Miss Poole. Promise me. For Shauna."

"I promise," said Odelia, touched. "I will leave no stone unturned."

## CHAPTER 35

Odelia was right: the secret passageway we'd discovered connected all of the rooms on our floor. Dooley and I had set out to explore them, and before long we'd discovered we could go literally anywhere and not be detected. Of course the rooms were all deserted now, with their inhabitants either having breakfast or being interviewed by Chief Alec's people, or even walking their dogs outside. Suddenly we heard voices, though, and so we followed them to the source. They were all male voices, so I was curious to say the least.

"Do you think we've hit upon a secret gathering within the secret passageways?" asked Dooley excitedly.

"No idea, Dooley."

"There could be a secret cult living within these walls, studying the people in the rooms, and murdering with absolute impunity," he said, his imagination taking sudden flight. Dooley is prone to such flights of fancy.

"Or it could be the cleaners taking a break," I said.

"That doesn't sound as exciting as my idea."

No, it certainly did not.

The voices appeared to originate from inside the room that had been awarded to Kimberlee's boyfriend upon Kimberlee's tragic demise. From what I could tell there were at least five occupants in there, yapping away.

Dooley and I positioned ourselves near the cracks in the wall so we had a perfect vantage point to spy on these humans without them knowing. I saw Kimberlee's boyfriend Zoltan, Emerald's husband Pete, Abbey's husband Seger, Verna's husband Thaw, and Alina's husband Reinhart. Even the director, Odo Hardy, was there. They were seated in the apartment's salon, drinking hard liquor and smoking something that smelled extremely... pungent.

"Weed," I told Dooley. "They're smoking weed."

"Why would they smoke weeds?" asked Dooley.

"Not weeds. Weed. It's a drug."

"A drug!"

"Humans like it. A lot of them seem to smoke it."

"So weird," was Dooley's determination. "Why would anyone want to fill their lungs with smoke? That just seems like a very irrational thing to do."

"I know, right?"

"I'm just saying, we gotta get out of this place," said Thaw. "No offense to you, Pete, or your lovely wife and your fabled hospitality, which is amazing, to be honest."

"Amazing," echoed Zoltan.

"And the food. Oh, my God." He kissed his fingers for some reason. "To die for, man. But there's cops crawling all over. And now with this maid that tumbled down the stairs..."

"Bad luck," Pete said. "First Kimberlee, now this. Why does this keep happening to us?"

"It's like that story from the bible," said Seger. "You get seven good years followed by seven lean years. Your luck will turn, buddy." He clapped a dejected-looking Pete on the shoulder. "Soon you'll prosper again."

"Maybe we should just sell the house," said Pete now. "After what happened it just doesn't feel the same."

"Don't do that!" said Reinhart. "If you sell now you'll get shafted."

"And if we stay we're screwed. We'll be social outcasts. And I'm not blaming you, Thaw. I wouldn't want to stay in a place where a woman just killed herself and another died in a freak accident."

"Yeah, that was pretty weird," said Seger. "What are the odds?"

They all sat in silence for a moment, then Odo Hardy held up his glass. "A toast. To Kimberlee. An amazing woman. And a once-in-a-lifetime talent."

"A toast," Pete said, holding up his glass.

The others all joined in. "To Kimberlee," said Zoltan sadly.

"To Kimberlee," the others echoed, and clinked their glasses.

"Looks like they all loved Kimberlee," said Dooley.

"Appearances can be deceiving," I told him. "One of these men may have killed two women in the last twenty-four hours."

"Pity we can't look inside their heads. Like a mind reader?"

"Yeah, wouldn't that be something?"

"Do you hear that?" suddenly asked Pete.

"What?" said Reinhart.

"Sounds like a cat. It's coming from over there."

"Uh-oh," I said. "Looks like we're busted, Dooley."

"Run, Max, run!" Dooley cried, and set the example by breaking into a run himself.

I quickly followed suit. I did not want to be caught by

these people. Spies are notoriously shy, and hate to be inter-rupted when they're spying on people, and cats are no different.

"There's nothing there, you guys!" we could hear Seger say. "Probably just the wind in the pipes!"

We hurried back to the room, flying like the wind—without the pipes—and popped out to safety, panting heavily, then laughing at our crazy adventure.

"That was fun," I said.

"Where did you guys go off to?" asked Harriet, who was perched on the bed, reading on Odelia's tablet computer.

"Exploring these secret passageways," said Dooley. "They run all over this floor."

"It's how the killer got into Kimberlee's room," I added. "Unseen and unheard."

"Except by the maid," said Dooley.

"So what are you up to?" I asked, hopping onto the bed. Or at least I tried to hop. The beds were pretty high, but I finally managed at my third attempt.

"Oh, just going through the pictures Odelia took of the crime scene," said Harriet, as if it was the most normal thing in the world.

"And? Have you found anything?"

Brutus, lying next to Harriet, was licking his fur. "Nothing so far," he said.

"Odelia asked us to take a look, just in case she missed something," said Harriet. She deftly flicked though the pictures with her paw pads.

Thank God for Steve Jobs. He's the one who made it possible for cats to use tablet computers and smartphones. Our pink pads are simply perfect for the purpose of scrolling through pictures or operating a touchscreen.

"That's the stack of Coke Emeralds," I said when a picture popped up depicting a pyramid of Coke cans.

"That's not the crime scene, though, right?" asked Dooley.

"No, just random pictures Odelia took when she and Chase first arrived here yesterday." Harriet suddenly narrowed her eyes, then expanded the picture for a closer look. "Now isn't that the weirdest thing?" she muttered.

"What is?" I asked.

Instead of responding, she quickly flicked through the pictures until she got to one of the can of Coke Kimberlee had drunk from. It was on the floor, next to the poor unfortunate woman's body.

Once again, Harriet zoomed in on the can. "You guys," she said finally, "I-I think I found something. I-I think I found—I've found a clue—an actual clue!"

# CHAPTER 36

When Odelia finally returned to her room, she hadn't learned much. She'd talked to some more people on staff, but no one had any idea about what Shauna could possibly have seen. Most of them simply held that the girl was delusional, and thought she was just trying to make herself look important by professing to hold some important piece of information.

So Odelia decided to take a break and check up on her cats and Gran, and when she entered her room wasn't disappointed. Four cats looked extremely excited, and so did her grandmother.

"They found something!" Gran said. "They found an important clue—or at least I think it is."

Odelia joined them on the bed, where all attention seemed to be centered on her tablet.

"So what did you find?" she asked with an indulgent smile.

"Actually it's Harriet who found it," said Max. "She's a genius."

This surprised Odelia. Usually Max was the sharpest of her small menagerie of cats, with Harriet too self-involved to make big contributions and Brutus too much trying to please Harriet to pay attention to much else. As far as Dooley was concerned, he was a sweetheart, but not the smartest cat.

"Look," said Harriet, flipping through the pictures on her tablet. "See these Coke cans?"

She saw the Coke cans. "Uh-huh."

"Now look closer." Harriet zoomed in on one of the cans. It looked like a regular can of Coke to her, only with the name Emerald added. "See?" said Harriet triumphantly.

"You have to show her the other pictures first," said Gran.

"What have you been up to, by the way?" Odelia asked her grandmother.

"I had a massage!" said Gran, chipper. "And a facial. Abbey suggested it to me. Apparently Emerald has her own private beauty salon, and since these people have nothing to do right now, because of all of the hullaballoo, I figured this was my chance. I'm going back there in ten for a mani-pedi."

Odelia cocked an eyebrow at her gran. "Good for you."

"Right?" She beamed genially at Odelia.

"Look, Odelia, look," said Harriet, trying to draw her attention.

"I'm looking, honey," she said. It was a picture of yet another can of Coke. "So what am I looking at, exactly?"

"This is the Coke Kimberlee drank from. The one with the poison?"

"Okay."

"Now look closer." Harriet zoomed in again, this time on the logo and more specifically the name Emerald.

"See?" she said triumphantly. "My clue!"

"Um... actually..."

"The picture!"

She frowned and then finally saw it. This can had a tiny picture of Emerald interposed on top of the E of Emerald.

"Don't the other cans have this?" she asked.

"No, they don't. So you see, this can is different from the others."

"I still don't see…"

"Remember how Brutus and I went exploring in Emerald's apartment? And how we saw a huge stack of Coke cans? Her own private stash? Well, they all had these tiny pictures of Emerald on them, while the stack of cans in the dining room don't."

"So… the can Kimberlee drank from came from Emerald's private stash," she said slowly.

"It did! Don't you think that's an important clue?"

"This could literally mean anything," she said, not wanting to disappoint Harriet but not wanting her to get carried away either. "This could simply mean that Kimberlee was in Emerald's apartment and took one of the cans."

"But don't you see—this is Emerald's private stash. Obviously she wants to keep these to herself."

"What I think happened," said Gran, "is that Emerald paid a visit to Kimberlee, coming in through the door, gifting her this special can, watched Kimberlee drink the cyanide-laced Coke and then got out through the secret passageway. Why else would Kimberlee have a can of Emerald's private stash in her room?"

Odelia shrugged. "Like I said, she could have been in Emerald's room, or Emerald could have given it to her as a special gift. She appointed Kimberlee her successor—said she wanted to see her succeed and be the heir to her throne."

"Who else would know about these secret passageways but Emerald?" said Max.

"Just about anyone. Just because Emerald didn't tell us

about those passageways doesn't mean she didn't tell the others."

"Kimberlee's doggie Stevie said Kimberlee and her mystery visitor—probably a woman—discussed a director role for Kimberlee for her next project," said Gran. "Emerald has been quoted as saying she's thinking about retiring from acting and turning to directing. She has also been quoted as saying she's looking for suitable actors." She held up her phone. "It's on the Internet!"

Odelia took Gran's phone. She'd found an article where Emerald did indeed talk about retiring from acting and becoming a director.

"Look, taken by themselves, the Coke clue isn't conclusive, nor is the passageways thing, or the directing thing," said Gran. "But together? I think you need to take a long, hard look at Emerald. I think she's our killer."

Odelia nodded slowly. Gran was right, and so were the cats. Taken together, Emerald was starting to look more and more like the person they'd been looking for.

"Those voices we heard last night?" said Max. "That must have been Emerald and Pete. And if Shauna came to deliver the note, and slip it under the door, Emerald could have seen her, and known the jig was up."

"This is all very circumstantial," said Odelia, gesturing to the tablet and the phone. "So how do we prove it?"

Gran smiled. "That's up to you, honey. I'm sure you'll figure it out. You are, after all, a great detective, if I say so myself." She picked up her phone. "And now if you'll excuse me, I have an appointment with a mani-pedi person." As she got up, she added, "First rule of show business: if you want to get the part, you have to look the part." And with these words, she was off.

"I think Gran would make a great diva," said Dooley.

"Yeah, she definitely has the personality for it," Max agreed.

Odelia found herself staring at the Coke can, and more specifically Emerald's face. "So how do I prove that you're the one?" she muttered.

# CHAPTER 37

*J* wasn't entirely happy with the role I'd been given in this, Odelia's idea for finally figuring out if Emerald was the person who'd killed her colleague. And I could tell that Dooley wasn't too thrilled with her idea either.

Harriet, on the other hand, was super-excited. Not only had she discovered the telling clue—the one clue that ruled them all, so to speak—but she'd been cast for a vital role in the next part of the drama. Brutus, of course, felt that his part was the most important one, and didn't stop reminding us of this.

"Look at it this way, guys," he said, spreading himself on the foot of the bed as if he owned it. "There are fighters in this world, and then there are pussies. You guys," he said, indicating me and Dooley, "are pussies, and so are you, darling," he added with a smile to Harriet. "But in a good way."

"Thanks, sugar plum," she cooed.

"Let me guess," I said. "And you're a fighter, right?"

"You got it, Maxie, baby. I've got the strength, I've got the speed, and I've got the stamina to see this thing through. You

204

guys, on the other hand, do not." He poked my belly. "Will you look at that? Pure flab. And you," he said, touching Dooley's non-existent belly, "skin and bones. Now feel my belly. Go on, give it a poke."

I gave him a very enthusiastic poke that made him wince.

"Feel that?" he said. "Pure muscle. Human males may boast about their six-pack abs, but I've got them all beat. I've got twelve-pack abs!"

"Twelve-pack abs?" This was the most ridiculous thing I'd ever heard.

"Sure! With a cat like me you get two for the price of one. Twice the killer instinct, twice the fatal attraction, and of course… twice the six-pack."

"Two six-packs. Really."

"Hey—Maxie can count! Congratulations, buddy!"

Brutus was obviously his usual obnoxious self again. I should have been thrilled but I wasn't. I preferred Brutus when he was down and out for the count. At least he wasn't as insufferable as he was now.

"So to tell you the truth I don't know what you guys are doing here. I told Odelia I can handle this and I can!"

We were in Odelia and Chase's room, where Odelia was currently holed up in bed, pretending to be fast asleep. I wasn't entirely sanguine about the whole setup, and Brutus babbling on and on didn't make me feel any better about it.

"Can you guys please be quiet?" finally asked Odelia. "You're going to scare her off."

"Action hero," Brutus whispered, pointing to himself. "Pussy," he added, giving me a final prod. "No offense, buddy."

"None taken," I muttered.

Time crept by ever so slowly, and I had the feeling we'd been there for hours and hours already.

"I have to tinkle," said Harriet suddenly. "Can I go tinkle?"

"Of course you can go tinkle," said Odelia. "But make it quick."

Harriet hopped off the bed.

"I have to go, too," said Dooley. "Can I go, too?"

"Oh, Dooley," said Odelia with a sigh.

The unfortunate thing was that Gran, due to space constraints, had only brought along a single litter box. And since she hadn't really paid a lot of attention she'd simply grabbed the first one she saw, which, of course, was Harriet's. And since Harriet is always very prissy about her litter box, now each time we wanted to go we had to ask her permission.

"Harriet, can I go tinkle?!" Dooley yelled.

"Yes, but only if you tinkle inside the box," Harriet yelled back. "No tinkling on the carpet. And don't you dare tinkle on the side of the box! No spillage!"

"I never tinkle on the side," said Dooley.

I sometimes tinkle on the side, but that's because I'm so big. Hey, it's not that I have bad aim, but they make these litter boxes awfully small.

Harriet returned and gave Dooley a censorious look. "Don't tinkle on my tinkle spot," she warned him. "That tinkle spot is my tinkle spot alone."

"Yes, Harriet," he said dutifully.

And of course when one cat has to go, they all have to go, so the moment Dooley returned it was my turn to go, quickly followed by Brutus.

"I think I need to go number two," Brutus said.

"No way," Harriet said. "Hold it in."

"I can't!"

"Odelia!" Harriet cried. "Please change the litter in my litter box as soon as Brutus is done."

"I'm not going to change the litter in your litter box each

time one of you does number two," said Odelia, starting to sound as if she was in a bad mood.

"Then you should have brought more than one litter box," said Harriet.

"I didn't even invite you guys here!" said Odelia. "This was all your idea!"

"Oh, for crying out loud, will you stop bickering!" a voice sounded from inside the wall.

It was Gran.

"I'm getting rheumatism from sitting on this chair for so long and I'm going deaf from all the bickering. When is this killer going to show her face?!"

"I'm not even sure she will show her face!" Odelia yelled back.

"I'm going to bed," said Gran. "This is ridiculous."

"Yeah, Ma, you better go to bed," another voice piped up, also from inside the wall. It was Uncle Alec. Like Gran and Odelia and the rest of us, he was waiting for the killer to finally make a move and show her face.

"Why? Don't you think I can do this?" asked Gran.

"You just said you want to go to bed, so go to bed already!"

"Well, I changed my mind. I'm staying put."

"Stay put, go to bed, I don't care—but can you please be quiet?!" Uncle Alec bellowed. "You're scaring off the killer!"

"Well, she's not going to show her face if you all keep bickering," said Gran.

"Can you all just please shut the hell up?!" Chase said. He was sitting in a chair in the corner of the room, conveniently cloaked in darkness.

"You shut up," said Gran. "You're not even supposed to be here."

"That was for the sake of the killer, Ma," said Uncle Alec. "Chase is part of the plan."

"And what a plan it is," she muttered. "Okay, fine, I'll shut up," she added when her son cleared his throat menacingly.

"Wow," said Brutus, finally returning from his bathroom break. "Don't go near the litter box if you don't want to suffocate."

"Brutus, eww!" Harriet cried.

"Yeah, Brutus," I said. "Too much information."

"Cats," said Dooley. "Twice the fun. Twice the smell."

We all laughed at that, until Gran bellowed, "Quiet!"

All was quiet, then, and soon I could hear the slow, even breathing of Odelia, as she drifted off to sleep. From inside the wall, I could hear Uncle Alec's soft snores, and Gran's louder snores, and from Chase's position I could tell he'd had a visit from the sandman, too.

"Sounds like they've all gone to sleep," said Harriet.

"Pussies," said Brutus. "Humans are pussies."

"So where is this killer?" asked Dooley.

"No idea," I said. "Maybe she won't even come."

"Bummer," muttered Brutus, rubbing his twelve-pack.

Nothing stirred, and soon even Brutus and Harriet had dozed off, and finally Dooley. According to my inner clock it was way past midnight, and I had a feeling this killer wasn't going to show up. So I closed my eyes and got ready for a healing nap myself, when suddenly a soft noise alerted me that something was up.

My eyes picked up movement in a corner of the room: the secret door had swung open and a person, clad in black from top to toe, had crept into the room. I gulped slightly as I watched the figure creep up to the bed. For a moment they simply stood there, watching on, and taking in the scene, then, when they were satisfied the coast was clear, they picked up a pillow from the bed and moved in on Odelia.

It was only when the pillow was pushed down on Odelia's

face that I finally managed to overcome my temporary paralysis and jerk into action: I produced the loudest protracted yowl I was capable of, and then I was hurling myself at Odelia's attacker, claws outstretched, zooming through the air like a regular feline Bruce Lee...

# CHAPTER 38

*O*delia's eyes shot open the moment the pillow touched her face. She jerked upright, and for a moment was dazed and confused. In spite of her best intentions she'd fallen asleep, and it took her mind a few seconds to get with the program.

There was a dark-clad figure screaming on the bed, and she could hear sounds of hissing and tearing of cloth. She quickly switched on the light and found herself the witness of an unusual scene: Max was fighting a nighttime marauder, who was making valiant attempts to ward off this feline attack!

The noise of the fight must have alerted the others, for suddenly the room was ablaze with light and movement, as Chase descended upon the bed, and from all sides, it seemed, the walls opened and Gran and Uncle Alec came running up. The cats, too, were wide awake, and were helping Max defeat this attacker by digging their claws into him or her.

But Chase was already subduing the person, and when Odelia said, "It's okay, Max—Max, you can let go now," he retracted his claws and retreated.

Chase, meanwhile, had stripped off the attacker's bala-clava, revealing the face of... Abbey Moret!

"Abbey?" Odelia said. "What the hell..."

"Let go of me, you big brute!" Abbey said, then found herself looking into the faces of Uncle Alec and Gran, who were equally stunned.

"She was trying to kill you, Odelia," said Max. "She was trying to put a pillow over your face and choke you."

"So it was you," said Odelia, still shocked. "You killed Kimberlee."

Abbey blew a strand of blond hair from her brow, then examined a nasty cut on her arm, where Max must have dug his teeth in.

"Those cats of yours are wild!" she complained. "You should keep them on a leash, like a normal person."

"My cats just saved my life," said Odelia, her heart still beating a mile a minute, adrenaline coursing through her veins.

"You had no clue, did you?" said Abbey bitterly. "When you went around during dinner, proclaiming you knew who killed Kimberlee and were going to reveal it to the cops in the morning. You were simply bluffing."

"I was," Odelia conceded. "But it worked, didn't it? You're here."

"Yeah, I'm here, and so are your cronies," she said, subjecting Chase, Gran and Uncle Alec to some particularly nasty side-eye.

"Better start talking," said Uncle Alec. "Why did you kill Kimberlee?"

For a moment it seemed as if Abbey was going to hold out, but then she relented. "Oh, I guess it's no use. Kimberlee was inching her way to the top by any means necessary, and one of those means was my precious husband."

"Seger? This is about Seger?" asked Odelia, surprised.

Abbey nodded. "He's one of the top talent agents in the business. He makes or breaks careers and Kimberlee wanted him to make hers. Only he didn't think she had what it took so he declined to take her on as his client. So she hired a private detective to dig around in his past and found some damaging little thing he did years and years ago. If he wouldn't launch her into the big time, she was going to expose it and destroy his life and, in the process, probably mine, too, as these things have a habit of spreading like wildfire and taking down everyone who's tainted by association."

"What secret?" asked Odelia.

She frowned and shook her head, indicating she wasn't prepared to tell them.

"We'll find out," said Alec.

"I'll bet you will," Abbey said ruefully. "Kimberlee had Seger in her pocket and was starting to make some frankly unreasonable demands. If he kept pushing her his own career was going to suffer. Everyone complained about Kimberlee, on every set of every project she got involved in, and it was starting to affect the way people viewed Seger. This is a business of trust. If Seger pushes an actress who can't deliver and makes a nuisance of herself wherever she goes, people are going to start asking questions, and pretty soon she was going to drag my husband down with her. So I did what I had to do."

"You set up the meeting and you killed her."

Abbey nodded. "It wasn't hard. I hated her guts with a vengeance. Not only did she use Seger, but she also came on to him, and when he refused, started pestering him even more. She was a jerk."

"Where did you get the cyanide?"

"On a movie set in Lithuania a couple of months ago. The sound guy was former Russian intelligence. He had a couple of cyanide pills from his days in the service and gave them to me as a present. In case I ever got fed up with my director. He only said it half in jest. The director on that shoot really was a terrible pest. So I put some of that cyanide in a Coke can and gave it to Kimberlee. She loved Coke Emerald, and especially since this was from Emerald's personal stash, which has just that extra kick the others lack."

"How did you get your hands on that can?"

"Emerald gave it to me—in fact she gave each of us a can of Special Coke Emerald: Kimberlee, me, Verna, Alina... So when I was in there, I offered Kimberlee mine and then when she was dead, I took hers so people would simply figure she'd killed herself."

"How did you get her to drink it?"

"She was a Coke addict. Easily downed a gallon a day. I went in there to talk about a new project Seger was setting up for her—she was eager to direct her own movie and he'd found a producer who was willing to take a chance on her—and to discuss the stuff that had just gone down with Alina. I said I hated Alina as much as she did, and she just gobbled it up. Started thinking up ways and means of murdering Alina in the most gruesome way possible. Ironically enough she was drinking a lethal dose of cyanide as she sat there fantasizing about killing Alina."

"How did you know about the secret passageways?"

"Emerald showed them to us last year. Said we could use them to sneak into each other's rooms for slumber parties and if we got tired of our husbands."

"What about Shauna?"

She frowned. "Who?"

"The maid you pushed down the stairs."

"Oh, that." She shrugged. "I think she saw me. She was in my room when I stepped out of the wall, right after Kimberlee was killed. It probably didn't take her long to put two and two together. So when I saw her shove that note under your door I just figured it was time to end her. So I did."

It was hard to believe that a woman who appeared so utterly sweet and kind could turn out to be such a ruthless killer, Odelia thought.

"And to think I liked you," she said finally.

"Oh, but I like you, too, honey," said Abbey, putting a hand on Odelia's arm. "But it's every woman for herself in this business. And it was pretty obvious to me you knew something, so you had to be silenced."

"It was you and Seger I heard talking last night, wasn't it? You were saying how careful you'd been and he was expressing his concern."

"Yeah, Seger knew, of course. Hard to keep something like that a secret from your husband. I caught him staring at pictures of Kimberlee yesterday. Can you believe that? His tormentor and blackmailer. Apparently he'd developed a crush on her after all. Stockholm syndrome, maybe. Anyway, he was worried somebody would find out. Seger has always been a worrier," she said with a wistful smile. "He's not going to be happy I got caught." She frowned. "And by a bunch of stupid cats."

CHAPTER 39

*W*e were finally home again, and seated on our favorite porch in Marge and Tex's leafy back-yard. The sun was setting, but the day was still nice and warm, and our favorite humans had all gathered for a Poole family tradition. A nice grill was sizzling, Tex had strapped on his apron and was officiating the grill, and Marge and Gran had just brought out the coleslaw and potato salad and if I knew Marge, a chocolate cake was in the fridge. Us cats were also in for a treat, as we got to snack on morsels of real meat for a change, as opposed to our kibble and wet food pouches that were our usual menu.

"I still don't get it," said Dooley. "Why would Abbey go to all this trouble—risk her career and her life—to get rid of Kimberlee?"

"Because Kimberlee had a secret she held over her husband's head like the sword of Damocles," I said. When Dooley gave me a blank look, I explained, "Kimberlee was blackmailing Seger with a secret from his past."

"I know all about that—but what secret could be so big to make him do what she told him to?"

215

"Uncle Alec figured that out," I said as I chewed on a tasty veal patty. "Apparently Seger was involved in a hit-and-run accident when he was a teenager. His dad was a prosecutor at the time and managed to bury the police report. Kimberlee had gotten wind of it and threatened to reveal the truth. It would have killed Seger's career and tarnished that of his dad. So he preferred to take Kimberlee on as a client rather than have her destroy his career."

"She was not a nice person," said Dooley judiciously.

"No, she was not."

"I solved the case," said Harriet, who was lying next to me. "I actually cracked this case. I'm the one who found the telling clue."

"Well, it wasn't exactly the telling clue," I said, then, when she gave me a censorious look, I quickly changed my tune. "It was a very important clue."

It was true. In a roundabout way it had led to the killer.

"I'm just glad it wasn't Emerald that did it," said Harriet. "I love Emerald. She's one of the biggest stars in the world. I hope she'll never stop acting."

"I bet she won't," I said. "A woman like Emerald can keep on acting until she's standing with one foot in the grave, and even then she'll make it fascinating to watch."

Out in the backyard, Chase was darting occasional looks in our direction, then shaking his head, a bemused grin on his face.

"I still can't believe you can actually talk to your cats," he told Odelia.

"You bet we can," said Marge, as she ladled more potato salad on her plate and dug in. "It's a blessing. How many cases have you solved this way, Odelia? A dozen? More?"

"Probably," Odelia said as she kept a close eye on her dad, who was spacing out again, at risk of allowing his burgers to burn to crisps.

"It's a blessing, and a curse," said Gran. "A blessing because it's a lot of fun to listen to those sweethearts and their conversation—they're like a bunch of toddlers—they just crack me up each time they open their little mouths."

"You know we can hear you, right?" I said.

She held up her hand. "And a curse because they just won't stop yacking. Day and night, they just go on and on and on. Yackety yackety yak. No end."

"That's it," Harriet snapped. "I'm not saying another word."

"Do we talk too much?" asked Brutus.

"Some of you talk more than others," Gran said, then pointed a finger at Harriet. "I'm not pointing fingers."

"She *is* pointing fingers, though," said Dooley.

"It's a human thing," I said. "They say one thing and mean something entirely different."

"It's very confusing."

"It is confusing," I agreed.

"I wish they wouldn't do that."

"Just let it go, Dooley."

"But I don't get it."

"See?" said Gran. "What did I tell you? Yackety-yak."

"It's fun, though," said Marge. "They're so much fun."

"I know, right!" said Gran. "That's my problem. I can't deny those furballs a thing. Anything they want, I give them. They're my Achilles heel."

Chase had wandered over and took a seat on the swing next to us. "So tell me, what do they say about me? Do they like me? Hate me? What?"

Marge and Odelia shared a look. "You don't want to know," said Marge.

"They think you're a great guy," said Uncle Alec.

"And how would you know?" said Gran. "You don't understand a word they say."

217

"I can tell from the expression on their faces," said Uncle Alec, taking a swig from his beer.

We all looked up at Chase, and I said reverently, "We think Chase is amazing."

"We think he's Jesus," said Dooley. "But without the sheep."

"He saved my life once," I said. "No, twice. Or is it three times?"

"He's the hunkiest male I've ever met," said Brutus. "Definitely not a pussy or a girly man like most. A man's man."

"Whatever that means," said Harriet with an eyeroll.

"It means he's my hero," said Brutus.

"I thought your hero was Caitlyn Jenner?" said Harriet. "You were going to change yourself into a woman, remember?"

"Oh, that was just a whim," said Brutus with a gesture of his paw.

"I wonder if Chase is neutered, just like we are," said Dooley now.

"He doesn't look neutered," said Brutus.

"How can you tell?" asked Harriet.

"I've seen him without his clothes," Brutus revealed. "He doesn't look neutered to me. He still has all his... assets. And they're quite formidable."

Harriet's eyes lit up with a renewed fervor. "He's not Jesus," she said now, reverently. "The man is a God. A superhero."

"Hey, and what am I? Chopped liver?"

"You're a demi-god, okay?" she snapped.

"I should have listened to Kingman," Brutus grumbled. "He told me there's a shop where they sell Neuticles."

"They sell what now?" I asked.

"Neuticles. Prosthetic testicular implants. They're made of silicone and look just like the real thing. They make them for neutered male pets, so they wouldn't feel so bad about having their appendages removed."

"Oh, just grow a pair," said Harriet, shaking her head.

"That's just it—I can't. But I can buy a pair."

"Oh, my god," she groaned.

"It's a thing!" said Brutus.

"Brutus, baby, when are you going to get it through that thick skull of yours that I don't care what you're packing? It's you I love, not your equipment."

"Oh, honey lamb," he said, mollified.

"Oh, snuggle pooh," she said.

Kissing ensued, and both Dooley and I rolled our eyes and looked away.

"If this is what birds and bees do, I'm not sure I want to know about it," Dooley said.

"I hear you, Dooley," I said. "I hear you."

"So?" said Chase blithely. "What's the verdict? Do they like me or do they like me?"

But Marge, Odelia and Gran were too busy rolling on the floor laughing.

That's one other thing us cats have: apart from the gift of the gab, we make people laugh.

And isn't that the greatest gift of all?

# EXCERPT FROM A GAME OF DONS (THE MYSTERIES OF BELL & WHITEHOUSE 10)

## Chapter One

Virgil Scattering had been walking for what felt like hours, and frankly he was starting to get a little tired. He might be a cop but that didn't mean he was a superhero. Then again, if he really was a superhero, he could have flown to his destination. Or he could have turned himself into a giant version of himself and taken one step to get where he was going, like Ant-Man. Unfortunately he wasn't Ant-Man but merely a humble human flatfoot, and therefore had to be content with using the power vested in his lower limbs.

He wiped his brow, which at this point was liberally covered with sweat, took a deep breath, and planted his fists in the small of his back as he took a little breather.

He wasn't built for strenuous physical activity. And especially not when the sun was burning down on him and temperatures were soaring. Once, in his younger years, as a beat cop just starting out, walking every corner of his town meant nothing to him. He walked them for fun and pleasure. Now, having just turned thirty, and after several years of dividing his time between filling out paperwork and driving to crime scenes, he was out of shape.

I should never have taken that call, thought Virgil now. A string bean of a man, with a battering ram of a chin, he wasn't exactly a model of physical beauty, but what he lacked in outward appeal he made up for in diligence. So when the call had come in that morning, he'd put down his donut— freshly baked at Bell's Bakery—and had listened intently to the voice of distress alerting him of something untoward going down on the other side of town.

"I need you to come down here, Virgil, and I need you to come now," the woman's voice had said with an urgency that had the hairs at the back of his neck pay attention.

"I'm sorry, who is this?" he'd asked, picking up a pencil and getting ready to jot down a few vital thoughts on what sounded like it might very well be a crime in progress.

"Robinson Street sixty-nine. Come alone and make sure you're not followed."

"I'm not—"

"Horse's head, Virgil. Horse's head, remember?"

He'd gulped and almost dropped the phone. "Horse's... head?" he'd repeated, a little hoarsely. "Is this... Miss Ko—"

"No names! You never know who's listening. Come alone —and whatever you do, don't mention this conversation to anyone. No one can know. Oh, and ditch the car."

"Ditch the—"

"Do I really have to say everything twice, Virgil? My God, you haven't changed, have you? Yes, ditch the car. Cars can be tracked—you should know. You're a cop. Come on foot and limber up your muscles. I've got a job for you and it involves physical exertion."

"Physical—"

"Just get here!" And she'd hung up, leaving him to stare at his phone in abject confusion.

"What's going on?" his colleague asked. Officer Louise Rhythm had recently been promoted to detective, and now occupied the desk directly across from his.

Virgil looked up. "I, um... I need to..." He'd abruptly gotten up.

"Virgil?" asked Louise, giving him one of her trademark 'has he just lost his frickin' mind?' looks. Her cornrows were perfectly coiffed, with some pink braided in today.

"I have to go," said Virgil, staring at Louise as if she'd just sprouted a second nose.

"Go where?" she asked emphatically, as if talking to a toddler.

"Um... out. On a case."

"I'm your partner, Virgil. Don't you think you should enlighten me about this case of yours? That way we can go together? As a team? Since that's what we are? A team?"

"Yes," he said, thinking hard, which was always a strain. "It's private," he said finally in a moment of snap illumination. "Um, like, a private case."

"A private case." She shook her head. "You're going down to Bell's Bakery again, aren't you? To get yourself some more of those delicious deep-fried goodies."

He pointed at her, relief flooding through him. "Yes! That's it! Goodies!"

"Bring me five, will you? Pink glaze and sprinkles. Oh, and some crullers."

He started to back away slowly. He wasn't used to lying to Louise. In fact he'd never lied to his partner in his life—or any of his colleagues—so this was all new. And weird.

"Virgil!" Louise called after him.

He froze. "Yes?"

She cocked her head. "Aren't you forgetting something?"

He gulped, eyes widening. This was it. Just like when Felicity Bell had discovered he'd stolen her Twizzlers in fifth grade. Ice touched his spine and his stomach did backflips.

She sighed audibly, then cocked her index finger at him. "Your gun and badge?"

"Oh, right!" Virgil said. He retraced his steps, reached into his drawer and retrieved the items under discussion, then quickly hurried off again, before Louise could stop him.

The moment his back was turned, he could hear her say, "One of these days he's going to forget to take his head."

He'd walked two miles, his shirt drenched and his feet aching, when he remembered the caller's words: make sure you're not being followed. So he looked left, he looked right, and he looked behind him. Apart from a child talking to herself while checking something on her phone, there was no one around. So he continued walking, at this point feeling as if he were training for a 24-hour challenge, and he wasn't even wearing his comfortable shoes.

Deanna Kohl. How about that? It had been years since he'd seen her last. Too many years to count. Last he heard she'd moved away to one of those fancy places in upstate New York. Places where a simple family home could set you back millions. Or was it billions?

He glanced around at the neighborhood he now found himself in. Grimey Hill had really gone downhill in recent years. Many of these older homes stood empty now, their owners having moved away. Weeds infested front yards, grass peeked through the cracks in the pavement, potholes littered the asphalt, and many of the houses were dilapidated.

He knew the area well. It was one of those eyesores that give a town council headaches. Most of the properties had been snapped up by a conglomerate of developers, with only a few homeowners stubbornly holding out. The neighborhood would be razed to make room for a housing tract. Virgil had even considered buying a home for himself here.

He still lived with his mom and from time to time was overcome with a sudden yearning for independence. His mom wouldn't be happy. She liked having a live-in son who did the odd chores around the house and kept burglars and salespeople at bay.

He arrived at the house in question. Yep. This was the place all right.

He took a deep breath, straightened his tie, and pushed through the wrought-iron gate, now rusted through. It clattered to the ground with a dull clunk. Virgil gulped. Bad sign.

He approached the front door, stepping over an ornamental stone frog that had stumbled off its perch, and pressed his finger to the bell. It didn't produce the merry tinkling one likes to hear in the suburbs. Instead it rasped like a bottle fly with smoker's cough. Inside, he could hear footsteps approach, and he arranged his features into the appropriate expression of professionalism and seriousness one likes to see in a cop making a house call.

The door creaked open and a woman appeared. There was a smudge of blood on her cheek and her eyes were a little wild, but she still looked as stunningly beautiful as ever.

"Oh, Virgil," she said, throwing her arms around him. "I thought you'd never show."

## Chapter Two

A black beetle walked across Alice Whitehouse's face. She could tell it was a beetle from the tiny little beetle feet tickling her cheek. Instantly awake, she threw back the covers with a mighty scream and kept on screaming even as she thrashed about, trying to remove the horrible bug from her face.

Immediately her housemates flocked to: Felicity, rushing in from the bedroom next door, along with Rick. Who didn't flock to was her bedmate, and when she looked over, she saw that he wasn't even there!

"What's going on?!" cried Fee.

"Yeah, what's with all the noise?" asked Rick, rubbing his stubbled cheek with a look of annoyance.

"There was something crawling on my face!" Alice cried, searching around frantically.

"What?" Fee squeaked. Like Alice, she didn't enjoy creepy crawlies invading her private space, especially when she was sleeping. "What was it? A spider? A mouse? A RAT?!"

"I think it was a black beetle," said Alice, now checking the comforter, which had fluttered to the floor. Fee picked up her pillow and started slapping it against the wall.

"You were probably dreaming," said Rick, ever the skeptic. Rick was a reporter. Being a skeptic came with the territory.

"I got him!" suddenly screamed Fee. "Kill him, Rick! Kill him!"

Rick turned to look, as did Alice. In plain view, right in the middle of Alice's Alice in Wonderland carpet, sat a black beetle of minute size. Still, it looked pretty horrible to Alice.

"No! Don't kill it!" she said even as Rick started to remove his slipper. "My carpet," she explained. "It's going to leave a stain. Besides... It's not right to kill the poor creature. He can't help it if he wandered into the wrong bedroom and onto the wrong face."

Or the right one if her act of benevolence was to be taken into consideration.

"Why don't you scoop him up in a little jar and put him outside, Rick?"

"If I put him outside he will simply come back in and then tomorrow night he'll be on my face," said Rick. "Or yours," he said, gesturing with his head to his girlfriend.

Fee shook her head violently, her mass of red curls

dangling. "I don't want him on my face. I can't have weird bugs on my face, Rick—do something!"

"He's not a weird bug," said Rick. "He's just a little beetle. Nothing weird about it."

"He's not little—he's huge!" said Fee.

"He's not huge. I've seen bigger beetles."

"He's horrible! Get rid of him—humanely," she added for Alice's sake.

"All right, all right. I'll put him in the backyard. He might like it so much he won't return to the scene of his most heinous crime of crawling all over Alice's face."

Alice shivered, but managed to say, "Thank you, Rick. You're the best." Speaking of the best, she wondered where her boyfriend was. "Where is Rock?" she now asked.

"Rock?" asked Fee with a frown. "Who's Rock?"

"You mean Reece," said Rick, searching around for a receptacle with which he could carry out his act of mercy.

Alice squeezed her eyes shut for a moment. "Um..." She vividly recalled her dream—as vividly as if it was real. Her boyfriend Reece Hudson, the hunky movie star, had fallen madly in love with Angelina Jolie and had dumped Alice. Not a tragedy, for she'd met an equally hunky male, a cop this time, working for her dad, and had happily dated him while solving crime in Happy Bays as the head of the Happy Bays Neighborhood Watch.

"Alice?" asked Fee. "Are you all right, honey?"

"It's the beetle," said Rick. "It gave her a big scare."

"I'm fine," said Alice. Or was she? That dream had seemed so real...

She became aware of water running in the bathroom, then being turned off.

A loud singing voice now intruded on the homey scene in the bedroom.

*"Shake it off—shake it off,"* the baritone sang slightly out of tune.

The three people present turned to the door when the singing grew louder. And then Reece strode in, a towel casually slung around his waist, water droplets clinging to his manly chest. He smiled broadly. "Hey, you guys. Got a little party going on in here, huh?"

A lifting sensation caught Alice by surprise. She actually teared up a little.

"Oh, Reece," she said.

Reece came over and wiped away a tear. "Hey, hey," he said. "What's the matter? Whatever it is, don't you worry about a thing. Reece is here to make it all better."

"I dreamed we broke up," she said, a slight lump in her throat.

"Broke up? Never."

"Yeah, we broke up when you fell in love with Angelina Jolie and then I got involved with a local cop."

"You got involved with Virgil?"

"No, his name wasn't Virgil. It was Rock... something." The dream was fading fast.

"Never heard of him," said Reece. He turned to Fee. "Who is this Rock dude?"

"No idea," said Fee with a shrug.

"Doesn't matter," said Alice with a smile, placing her hands on Reece's chest. "I'm so glad you're back."

"Back? I was never gone," said Reece. "And as far as Angelina Jolie is concerned, she can't hold a candle to you— my precious ladybug."

She smiled through her tears. "Ladybug. Now there's a beetle I like."

Rick cleared his throat. "So do you want me to catch your black beetle or not?"

Reece cocked an eyebrow at the beetle. It must have been

the sheer power of the actor's personality, for the offending little bug suddenly spread its wings, took flight, and zoomed straight out of the window!

Reece grinned and spread his arms. "Hot potato!"

## Chapter Three

Deanna looked as beautiful as Virgil remembered. She still had that gorgeous face with those high cheekbones, perfect bone structure, full lips, large eyes and perfectly coiffed blond hair. When he stepped into the house, following her into the living room, his heart skipped a beat— or maybe even two or three beats—and it was as if he was transported back to the moment he'd met her for the first time, as a cadet at police academy where she'd been his instructor.

Even then she'd been fully aware of her fatal allure and had done little to mitigate the impact of her shapeliness on her hormonal pupils. Virgil had been but one of many admirers, and he'd never even been aware that she'd been aware of him until that auspicious night in the swamp. The recruits called it the hellhole, because of the millions of mosquitoes that seemed to labor under the misapprehension that they were in charge, and that the cadets bused in for their nocturnal training were simply food items on the menu.

The recruits had been induced to crawl through the undergrowth in an exercise aimed at teaching subterfuge, camouflage and the skill of sneaking up on a suspect unseen and unheard. Virgil had quickly been both seen and heard, and by Deanna Kohl herself no less. He'd seen her first—or that's what he'd thought at the time—and had lain perfectly still. Finally, after a tense few minutes, Deanna had crouched down next to him.

"Scattering. I saw you five minutes ago. What the hell are you waiting for?"

"I, um, I thought I'd, um, stick around," had been his eloquent response. It had elicited a tinkling laugh from the instructor, and she'd patted his head affectionately, not unlike one would a favorite puppy.

"I like you, Scattering. You may not be police academy material, but you're funny. Now go and get your donut and hot cocoa and report back to HQ on the double."

"But..."

"The games are over for you, sonny boy. Now get."

And that had been the end of that. He'd later fantasized about spending a few more minutes chatting with Deanna Kohl in that undergrowth, imagining what could have been, but even then his self-esteem hadn't been all that much to write home about, and Deanna most definitely was way out of his league. So much so she inhabited a different universe.

He entered the living room and Deanna stepped aside, a thoughtful look on her face as she studied Virgil.

On the floor, spread out across the rug, lay the body of a large man. His shirt was unbuttoned, revealing a hairy barrel chest and protruding belly, and there was a hatchet buried in his throat, and a whole lot of blood pooled around his head.

Virgil swallowed. "He looks dead," he said.

"Your powers of observation are unparalleled," said Deanna. "Yes, he's dead."

"Did-did you do this?"

Deanna nodded slowly. "I could lie and tell you I didn't—but what's the use?"

"Who is he?"

"Who cares?"

"He kinda looks familiar."

He stared at the man for a moment, but a wave of nausea made him look away.

She extracted a pack of cigarettes from the recesses of her dress, and offered him one.

"No, thanks," he declined.

She shrugged and lit up. "It was an accident, of course."

Virgil sighed. "I don't know why you called me, Deanna," he said, even though he knew perfectly well why she'd called him.

She laughed a dry laugh, and flicked her ashes to the floor, hitting the dead man.

"Please don't do that," he said. "You're messing up the crime scene."

"And we're going to mess it up a lot more," she announced.

He gave her a look of surprise. "What?"

"You and I are going to dump this body where no one will ever find it, and then we're going to wipe this room clean. We're going to scrub and scrub until the last remnant of DNA of both him and me is gone forever. And do you know why we're going to do that, Virgil?"

He gulped. He had a pretty good idea. Still he asked, "Why?"

She smiled that infectious smile that had made his heart beat a little faster when he'd seen her answer the door just now. "Because you owe me."

He sagged down onto a chair, draping his boneless limbs across the piece of rickety furniture like a damp rag. "Yes, I do," he admitted. And now he was going to pay. Big time.

# ABOUT NIC

Nic Saint is the pen name for writing couple Nick and Nicole Saint. They've penned novels in the romance, cat sleuth, middle grade, suspense, comedy and cozy mystery genres. Nicole has a background in accounting and Nick in political science and before being struck by the writing bug the Saints worked odd jobs around the world (including massage therapist in Mexico, gardener in Italy, restaurant manager in India, and Berlitz teacher in Belgium).

When they're not writing they enjoy Christmas-themed Hallmark movies (whether it's Christmas or not), all manner of pastry, comic books, a daily dose of yoga (to limber up those limbs), and spoiling their big red tomcat Tommy.

www.nicsaint.com

## ALSO BY NIC SAINT

**The Mysteries of Max**

Purrfect Murder

Purrfectly Deadly

Purrfect Revenge

Box Set 1 (Books 1-3)

Purrfect Heat

Purrfect Crime

Purrfect Rivalry

Box Set 2 (Books 4-6)

Purrfect Peril

Purrfect Secret

Purrfect Alibi

Box Set 3 (Books 7-9)

Purrfect Obsession

Purrfect Betrayal

Purrfectly Clueless

**Nora Steel**

Murder Retreat

**The Kellys**

Murder Motel

Death in Suburbia

**Emily Stone**

Murder at the Art Class

**Washington & Jefferson**

First Shot

**Alice Whitehouse**

Spooky Times

Spooky Trills

Spooky End

Spooky Spells

**Ghosts of London**

Between a Ghost and a Spooky Place

Public Ghost Number One

Ghost Save the Queen

Box Set 1 (Books 1-3)

A Tale of Two Harrys

Ghost of Girlband Past

Ghostlier Things

**Charleneland**

Deadly Ride

Final Ride

**Neighborhood Witch Committee**

Witchy Start

Witchy Worries

Witchy Wishes

**Saffron Diffley**

Crime and Retribution

Vice and Verdict

**The B-Team**

Once Upon a Spy

**Tate-à-Tate**

Enemy of the Tates

**Ghosts vs. Spies**

The Ghost Who Came in from the Cold

**Witchy Fingers**

Witchy Trouble

Witchy Hexations

Witchy Possessions

Witchy Riches

Box Set 1 (Books 1-4)

**The Mysteries of Bell & Whitehouse**

One Spoonful of Trouble

Two Scoops of Murder

Three Shots of Disaster

Box Set 1 (Books 1-3)

A Twist of Wraith

A Touch of Ghost

A Clash of Spooks

Box Set 2 (Books 4-6)

The Stuffing of Nightmares

A Breath of Dead Air

An Act of Hodd

Box Set 3 (Books 7-9)

A Game of Dons

**Standalone Novels**

When in Bruges

The Whiskered Spy

**ThrillFix**

Homejacking

The Eighth Billionaire

The Wrong Woman

**Short Stories**

Felonies and Penalties (Saffron Diffley Short 1)

Purrfect Santa (Mysteries of Max Short 1)

Purrfect Christmas Mystery (Mysteries of Max Short 2)

Purrfect Christmas Miracle (Mysteries of Max Short 3)

Purrfectly Flealess (Mysteries of Max Short 4)